STAR WARS™

LANDO'S LUCK

WRITTEN BY

JUSTINA IRELAND

ILLUSTRATED BY

ANNIE WU

DISNEY
LUCASFILM
PRESS

LOS ANGELES · NEW YORK

Printed in the United States of America

First Edition, October 2018

1 3 5 7 9 10 8 6 4 2

FAC-020093-18240

ISBN 978-1-368-04150-8

Library of Congress Control Number on file

Reinforced binding

Designed by Leigh Zieske & Jason Wojtowicz

Visit the official *Star Wars* website at: www.starwars.com.

SUSTAINABLE FORESTRY INITIATIVE   Certified Sourcing
www.sfiprogram.org
SFI-00993

THIS LABEL APPLIES TO TEXT STOCK

For all of the space princesses . . . pew pew pew!

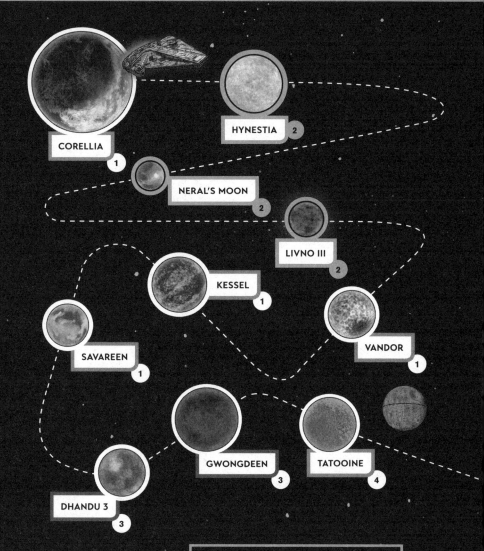

CORELLIA **1**

HYNESTIA **2**

NERAL'S MOON **2**

LIVNO III **2**

KESSEL **1**

SAVAREEN **1**

VANDOR **1**

GWONGDEEN **3**

TATOOINE **4**

DHANDU 3 **3**

FOLLOW THE ADVENTURE!

1 *Solo: A Star Wars Story*

2 *Lando's Luck*

3 *Pirate's Price*

4 *Star Wars: A New Hope*

5 *Choose Your Destiny: A Luke & Leia Adventure*

6 *Star Wars: The Empire Strikes Back*

7 *Star Wars: Return of the Jedi*

8 *Star Wars: The Force Awakens*

FLIGHT OF THE FALCON

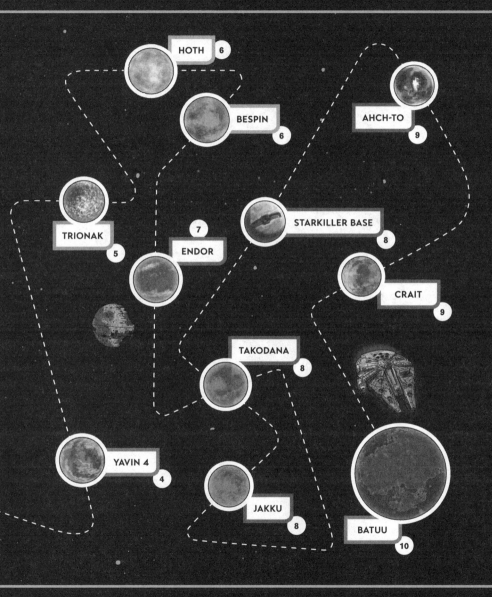

HOTH 6

BESPIN 6

AHCH-TO 9

TRIONAK 5

ENDOR 7

STARKILLER BASE 8

CRAIT 9

TAKODANA 8

YAVIN 4 4

JAKKU 8

BATUU 10

9 *Star Wars: The Last Jedi*

10 *Star Wars: Galaxy's Edge*

These titles and more available from

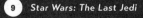

Disney

LUCASFILM PRESS

The Stinky Jawa Cantina on Vixnix, a small planet on the edge of Wild Space, was little more than a hole, but it was no worse than other places Bazine Netal had visited during missions for her various employers. Just a little less glamorous maybe. The music was subpar and the room was smoky, but the cantina hadn't been her choice. She would have to make the best of the situation and get what she needed before clearing out.

She adjusted her black cowl to make sure it was in place and straightened her baffleweave overcoat as she perched on a stool, watching people come and go. First impressions were important, and until she'd completed her mission, she had a part to play.

Hired spy? No. Interested recorder of history? That sounded better.

The message had said for Bazine to meet the contact in the cantina, at a table in the back right corner.

There'd been no description of her contact, and this was the third time Bazine had ended up in some backwater cantina on an anonymous tip. She hoped this one would pan out as something more than just a bunch of farmers imagining the most famous ship in the galaxy had crashed in their field.

Bazine had hoped to find her contact already in place when she'd arrived, but a casual stroll around the cantina earlier in the day had revealed only a single Ewok drinking a pitcher of purple glandis flower juice. Bazine had taken up position at the bar to watch the door for any potential marks, but there she was a few minutes to the appointed time and there still hadn't been any likely candidates. She didn't know whom she was supposed to meet, but she knew she was the first to show up.

Only when Bazine doubled back to the designated corner table, a woman sat there, a polite smile on her face. "I hope you didn't have trouble finding it," she said. Her brown skin was unlined, but gray streaked the long braids she wore. Her hazel eyes demanded a second look, and the woman raised a hand in greeting, not offering to shake when she noticed Bazine's fingertips. She did raise an eyebrow at the Rishi ink–stained digits.

"Strange attire for an archivist," the woman said. Her voice rasped, and Bazine frowned, trying to place the accent. The woman was definitely human, but she spoke like Basic wasn't the language she was used to.

"Are you the one who has a story for me?" Bazine asked, ignoring the comment and settling into the chair across from the woman.

"You're looking for information on a ship, are you not? A Corellian freighter, modified past its original intent?"

"I am," Bazine said. Perhaps the old woman was insane. There was an air to her that Bazine had seen before, mostly in travelers who spent too much time in Wild Space, away from the more civilized parts of the galaxy. All those stars could sometimes make people lose track of themselves. Bazine half expected the woman to jump up on the table and perform some kind of heavy, stomping dance in the mag-boots she wore. But the old woman stayed right where she was, her gold-green eyes watching Bazine in a way she found unsettling.

"Yes! Yes, I can tell you about a Corellian freighter. I can tell you about the *Millennium Falcon*."

Bazine straightened slightly—nothing that would be obvious to an outside observer, but inside she felt as though a string had been pulled taut. She'd never said the name of the ship, and her initial contact hadn't mentioned it in his message. But there it was, all the same.

The *Millennium Falcon*. A ship, a wreck of one from what she could tell. But one that had long been whispered about the way some still whispered of the Sith Lords and their bygone deeds. And this woman knew of it.

"What can you tell me about this ship? About this *Millennium Falcon*?" Bazine asked, drumming her inky fingertips on the surface of the sticky table.

"What can you tell me about payment?" the woman asked. Bazine reached under her coat and produced a bag holding a thousand credits, then dropped it on the table. A hulking shape, slightly larger and taller than Bazine, appeared. She got the quick impression of tufted ears, three tails, and fur that shifted color before the unknown alien grabbed the bag of credits and ambled off, disappearing into the shadows of the cantina. The entire exchange took mere seconds. The woman smiled.

Bazine was impressed. Not only had the woman managed to enter the Stinky Jawa without Bazine seeing her, she'd managed to bring an entourage.

Who was she?

"I know the *Millennium Falcon*. I know it well. Even flew it once," the woman said, laughing at some far-off memory.

"When did you first see the ship?" Bazine asked, feeling as though the world were shifting slightly every few moments, as though she stood on the deck of a sea craft instead of sitting in a cantina on a deserted backwater planet. The woman made her uneasy.

"Long ago, when I was a girl." The woman's eyes lost

focus as she drifted off into memory, a slight smile on her face. Bazine started the recorder under her coat, but the woman didn't seem to notice. She was already caught up in the spinning of the tale.

"It was a beauty of a ship then, refurbished by a man who loved that ship almost more than he loved anything but himself," the woman said. "A smuggler who went by the name of Lando Calrissian."

Lando Calrissian looked at his cards one last time and sat back in his chair. He stroked his mustache, smoothing it so each and every hair lay perfectly flat. Lando liked to look good when he won. He was, after all, building a legend.

Anyway, there was no point trying to hide his pleasure; the hand was almost over and the bets had been laid. Earlier in the evening Lando had wondered about his luck as he lost hand after hand, but it seemed like it had changed for the better. The Quarren female across the way kept looking at her dwindling pile of creds and then back at the cards in her hand in a way that could only be described as worried. The Lynna sitting to the left of Lando had started to groom herself, running her paws nervously over the wide tufted ears on top of her head. Her gray-and-black-striped fur was already immaculate, and the last time she'd begun to groom herself, she'd had the worst hand of the evening.

Lando was about to win, and he hadn't even had to cheat.

Well, not much, at least.

Someone entered, and a chill passed through the cantina, the frigid air making Lando wrap his cape a little closer to his body. Hynestia wasn't much of a planet, cold and wintry, a frozen tundra of a place with only a small zone of habitable land toward the equator. But Hynestia was known throughout the galaxy for its gherlian fur, a thick pelt that came not from an animal but a curious sort of lichen that Hynestians cultivated in domes built across the frozen landscape. It was a commodity tightly regulated by the Empire since it had claimed the planet for its own, which made the fur even more desirable. The more something was kept from people, the more they wanted it. And the more that people wanted a thing, the more they were willing to pay for it.

Lando was always willing to help. For a fee, of course.

It was the gherlian fur that had brought Lando to Hynestia. He had a lead on a particularly valuable relic that a collector was willing to part with for the right price. That price happened to be a crate full of gherlian pelts. And since there was only one place in the galaxy to get gherlian, Lando and his best droid, L3-37, had gone to Hynestia.

But no trip was complete without a few hands of Sabacc, especially when the *Millennium Falcon* was low on fuel and Lando was light on creds. And although Hynestia's lone cantina, the Frozen Kova, wasn't much—just a handful of tables and a single bar tended by a surly Mon Calamari—there were several games of chance going, and what more could a young entrepreneur want?

The Quarren stared at the pile of creds in the middle of the table and then at her cards again, her facial tentacles waving about in irritation. She let out a deep breath and threw her cards facedown on the table.

"Fold," she said, standing to leave. She towered over the Sabacc table, her blue-green skin glistening in the low light of the cantina. "And I think you've taken enough of my creds for one night, Calrissian."

"Well, I am sorry to see you go," Lando said with a respectful nod. She was an excellent player, and Lando always enjoyed playing against someone with skill. "But if you ever find yourself in this part of the galaxy again, Bweena, please stop by and say hello."

The Quarren made a blooping noise that was either agreement or a rude sort of retort. Either way, Lando just kept grinning. He was about to be a very rich man.

"And you, my dear," he said, turning toward the Lynna running a paw over her ears.

"Zel. Zel Gris. That's my name. Not 'my dear.'" The Lynna had a soft, husky voice that was at odds with her large size. "And I'm not out of it just yet."

Zel tossed a few more creds into the pile on the

table and exchanged a couple of her cards. It was her last exchange, and any worry that might have plagued Lando evaporated when her whiskers twitched once and then again.

She still held a terrible hand.

"Well, I suppose that's that," Lando said. He spread his cards across the table. "Pure Sabacc."

The Lynna heaved a sigh and stood to leave, her trio of tails swishing in irritation. Her gray stripes had shaded to a deep burgundy. Her wide shoulders slumped, and she towered over the table. "Bad luck, bad luck," she muttered as Lando cleared the creds off the table.

"Bad luck? No such thing," Lando said, laughing, even though he completely and utterly believed in luck—good, bad, and otherwise. But the Lynna was agitated, and Lando did not like it when people left his Sabacc table irate. Anger had a way of turning blasty, and Lando would rather smooth ruffled feathers—or fur, in this case—than deal with any unpleasantness later.

Zel gave Lando a look from the side of her eye that was somehow both insulting and dismissive, and turned to go. But something at the entrance of the cantina made her freeze.

"Oh, no. Bad luck. Worst luck," she muttered, the burgundy of her fur shading to a mustard yellow. She turned toward the back of the cantina, where a few folks snored, their cups of purple glandis flower juice mostly empty.

Lando watched her go and then turned back to the front of the cantina to see what had caused her sudden flight. It didn't take much to guess what had provoked her distress. A shadowy figure stood in the entry, the low light barely catching the gray and blue of the blaster he held. And even though Lando was quite smart, it didn't take a genius to spot a bounty hunter.

The man scanned the room. He wore a helmet, and the reflective visor hid his face, making him seem even more sinister. Lando didn't bother waiting to see if the bounty hunter was looking for him. He hurriedly pocketed the few remaining creds still on the table.

"Bad luck, indeed," Lando murmured. He stood and walked nonchalantly to the bar, his eyes on the bounty hunter the entire time. Sure, the hunter could be there for anyone, but only Lando had just smuggled in thirty barrels of purple glandis flower juice, a delicious drink that was quite illegal on Hynestia.

Lando was not a man to overstay his welcome, and between the skittish Lynna and the bounty hunter stalking through the cantina, it was a brilliant time to plan a departure. Besides, he had more than enough creds to fuel up the *Falcon* and several crates of gherlian furs secreted in his ship. The last thing he needed was trouble.

Lando grabbed his overcoat from a nearby hook and settled it into place nonchalantly before casually making his way to the door. He waved jauntily at the bartender as though they were old friends, and predictably the Mon Calamari burbled dismissively.

Lando schooled his expression to one of good cheer and walked toward the door. He was almost out of the cantina when his luck went completely south.

"Halt, Zel Gris!" the bounty hunter yelled. "I am here to apprehend you, and resistance is not recommended."

Lando turned to see the Lynna sprint across the room toward what must have once been a rear entrance but was now a blocked door.

The bounty hunter leapt across the cantina, vaulting tables and pushing patrons to the side. People shouted in dismay. A few patrons hurriedly grabbed their things and left, letting in swirls of snow in their hasty departure. Lando tried to join the fleeing fray, but someone grabbed a handful of his overcoat and yanked him backward.

"Not you, friend. Why don't you have a seat." A tall human woman with bright red hair and skin as pale as the Hynestia landscape pointed a blaster at him. She was dressed all in green in the traditional garb of the Hynestians: a thick gherlian overtunic belted around the waist and shiny leggings made of kova leather, which came from the skin of an underground reptile the Hynestians hunted for food.

Lando held up his hands and sank into the chair she indicated. "What would this happen to be about?" he asked with a cheerful grin.

"This would be about the purple glandis flower juice you smuggled onto Hynestia. The royal family doesn't like it when offworlders flaunt their laws."

"Oh, I'm afraid you have me confused with someone else . . ." Lando began, but drifted off when the woman shoved the blaster in his face.

"Sit there and be quiet," she said, and Lando pressed his lips shut.

Across the cantina, the bounty hunter had caught the Lynna and now held her captive. Zel's arms were locked to her body in restraining hoops, and her fur shaded to a sickly pale green. Lando felt ill just looking at her. The bounty hunter pulled out a chair and sat her next to Lando. The poor Lynna let out a single yowl of despair, and Lando sighed. He knew how she felt.

Everything had been going so well.

Rinetta Gan, Princess of Hynestia, First of Her Name and Scourge of the Royal Guard, was late. Again. She'd promised Zel Gris, her strategy instructor and favorite person in all the galaxy, that she'd meet her at the Frozen Kova cantina in exactly an hour, ready to leave. But there it was, ten minutes past when Rinetta was supposed to be at the cantina, and she was still looking for her boots.

All because she hadn't picked up her room like she was supposed to.

The heavy magnetic boots had been a gift from her mother, and even though Rinetta didn't always get along with her mom, they were her favorite boots in the world. They were perfect for all sorts of mischief, and there was little Rinetta liked more than going on an adventure.

That was why she had to hurry up and get to the cantina. Rinetta and Zel were going to save the world. Not Hynestia, maybe, but *a* world nonetheless.

If Rinetta could find her blasted boots.

There was a sudden knock on her door, and a member of the Royal Guard sauntered in.

"The royal Queen Mother, Forsythia Jin," the woman said. It wasn't Twyla, whose red hair and pale skin were hard to miss. This woman had short dark hair and skin so dark it reminded Rinetta of the night sky when neither of Hynestia's moons shone. She stood next to the doorway, and Forsythia Jin, queen of Hynestia and mother of Rinetta, strode into the room like a bad omen.

Rinetta loved her mother. But she also felt like she constantly disappointed her; so every time she saw Queen Forsythia, a vague sense of dread came over her. That day was no different.

"Hello, Mother," Rinetta said, dipping into the deep bow that was customary. As she bent down she spotted her mag-boots under a decorative end table, buried under a pile of school books. *Aha!*

"Rinetta, our honored daughter, we regret to inform you of some terrible news. Your beloved strategy instructor, Zel Gris, is a traitor." Queen Forsythia's long curly hair had been subdued into a series of braids that arced across her head in a complicated crown. Her deep brown skin shone with a dusting of golden powder, and her beauty made Rinetta too aware of the fact that her own braids were coming loose, a bit of fluff escaping the twists.

But then Rinetta realized what her mother had said and she straightened with shock. "Wait, Zel Gris is a traitor? How could this be?" Rinetta asked, feigning surprise. Her heart pounded so hard she was afraid her mother or the guard might hear it and see the lie for what it was, but neither of them moved.

Rinetta already knew Zel Gris had fled, possibly taking the Solstice Globe with her, but it wouldn't do for the queen of Hynestia to know, as well. That would ruin everything. Rinetta held her breath as her mind raced. What to do? She had to help Zel!

Rinetta's face must have shown some of her dismay, because the queen dismissed the lone guard and closed the door behind her. Once the guard was gone, the queen's expression relaxed. "Rinetta, I am so sorry. I know how much you cared about Zel. But she tried to steal the Solstice Globe before she fled."

Rinetta blinked, because she always found it a little difficult when her mother switched from her royal Queen Mother act to just being a mom. When Rinetta was younger, before the Empire arrived on Hynestia and demanded tribute and threatened to destroy them all if they didn't comply, she and her mother would take trips out to Wild Space to see the places her ancestors had traversed once upon a time, planets mostly undiscovered by the rest of the galaxy. Those trips had been fun and relaxed, and Queen Forsythia would tell Rinetta funny stories and show her amazing things.

But Rinetta rarely saw that side of her mother any-more. More often than not, Queen Forsythia spent her days closed up in her study, tracking the growth of the gherlian furs that would continue to buy Hynestia a limited amount of freedom from the Empire. So see-ing her now made Rinetta's stomach churn, because she was about to lie to her mother, the biggest lie she had ever told her.

"Solstice Globe? I don't know what that is," Rinetta said, trying to keep a confused expression on her face.

"It's a priceless artifact, but nothing you need to con-cern yourself with." The queen sighed and went to a nearby chair, pushing several gherlian fur tunics to the side before she sat down. "Actually, I should start tell-ing you these things. You're thirteen now, and should something happen to me, you would be queen."

A lump formed in Rinetta's throat. She hated when her mom talked like that, like she was going to up and die the next day. It made Rinetta very anxious, although that might be the lie that scratched at the back of her mind. *You should tell Mother the truth*, a voice whispered. Nonsense. She was doing the right thing.

"What is happening with the Solstice Globe?" Rinetta asked, pushing her guilt aside.

"Since our tribute to the Empire has been waylaid by thieves, we will be sending the globe along as pay-ment instead. Honestly, that orb is more trouble than it's worth. So many attempts to steal it over the years. Either way, the important thing here is Zel. She has betrayed our trust and tried to steal from the treasury. You're going to learn that you cannot trust people to do the right thing, and those you care about will disappoint you the most."

The queen's words burrowed into Rinetta like a parasite, and she fought to keep from confessing. Zel was doing the right thing, and maybe the queen couldn't see that because she was too worried about the tribute payment to the Empire. "Do you know where Zel is now?" Rinetta asked.

The queen shook her head, an uncharacteristic gesture. Rarely had Rinetta ever seen her mother look so . . . flustered. "I have the Royal Guard and a bounty hunter by the name of Xersko looking for her right now. She must be found and punished. But I wanted to let you know, my dear, before you learned of it from other sources."

Rinetta's heart picked up a triple beat of panic. Punishment took many forms on Hynestia, but the most severe was being fed to the Gran Kovali. It wasn't a pretty sight, and even though Rinetta had never seen anyone sentenced to death herself, there were dozens of records in the archive. None of them were pleasant.

Rinetta reached under the table and grabbed her mag-boots, pulling them on. "Mother, let me come with you, help you find Zel. I think it would be good training for me, to know how best to deal with criminals." Her mind raced, wondering if she could get to the cantina in time to warn Zel. It didn't sound like the queen had found Zel, yet, so maybe Rinetta could slip out of the palace and warn her friend before the bounty hunter discovered the Lynna.

Rinetta was very good at all kinds of mischief, and was even better at avoiding trouble.

But then the guard knocked loudly on the door and stuck her head in. "Exalted? The traitor has been found. The captain of the guard is requesting your presence to hand down a sentence."

Rinetta fought to hide her fear. She had to do something to make sure Zel would be spared. If only she'd gotten to the cantina in time.

That would teach Rinetta to leave her room a mess.

The door to the Frozen Kova cantina swung open once again, and several more men and women entered, the blustery wind and a few errant snowflakes entering with them. Most of the group wore the same green ensemble as the redheaded woman who had subdued Lando. But two of the women wore outfits of bright blue, and they looked to be related, mother and daughter perhaps. They both had skin the same deep brown as Lando's and hazel eyes, although the girl looked less certain about the situation than her mother. Worried, even. The older of the two women moved with a lethal grace. She entered the cantina and scanned it with the practiced air of an assassin, her expression neutral, her body tense, like she needed only the least provocation to spring into action. Once it was clear to her that the room held no threat, she removed her overcoat and tossed it on a nearby chair, the elaborate gherlian fur hat she wore going along with it. The woman's curly hair was twisted up in a complicated style that made Lando's heart sink.

He was no expert on Hynestia, but even he could tell a royal when he saw one. And there was only one royal left in the Hynestian royal family.

"Do you know who we are?" the woman asked Lando as she moved toward him.

Lando paused for a moment, looking around at the assembled group of men and women until he realized the woman was only talking about herself. He nodded slowly. He mulled over his words for a moment before deciding flattery was the best course of action, as usual. "By your beauty I'm thinking that you must be Forsythia Jin, the Assassin Queen."

The woman's neutral expression twisted into one of irritation. "Do not call us by that despicable title. We are Forsythia Jin, the savior of Hynestia. And you may call us Exalted, Lando Calrissian."

Lando hid his surprise that she knew his name and inclined his head respectfully, his expression schooled to show contrition. "Forgive me, Exalted. I meant no offense. Rather, I think it's admirable. The galaxy needs more women who stand by their convictions."

Lando's brain spun through a million different plans, with the hope that he could somehow get off-world in one piece.

Forsythia Jin was known as the Assassin Queen for

good reason. After her mother had died, leaving the crown in dispute, Forsythia had done everything necessary to ensure her claim was the only one. She had systematically killed every single competitor for the throne. The stories said she'd traveled the galaxy to find every last one of her twelve siblings, with the help of a bounty hunter, and had killed them with a ruthless precision that left onlookers stunned.

Lando learned all that during his research prior to setting foot on Hynestia. Over numerous evenings Lando had listened to the stories told by Hynestian refugees, servants, and retainers who had fled the planet when things turned violent. Lando had believed much of it to be exaggeration in the nature of all good stories. But looking at the Assassin Queen herself, Lando had no doubt those tales were true.

Especially since, shortly after taking her throne, Forsythia had faced down the Empire and made a deal that left her planet independent, if indebted. The Hynestians maintained their self-determination as long as they paid the Empire in gherlian furs twice a season. Lando had thought it was a raw deal, but now that he was in the presence of Forsythia Jin, he thought maybe the Empire had gotten the bad end of the bargain.

Forsythia Jin was not a woman to cross.

While Lando worked through all this, Forsythia turned her attention to the Lynna sitting next to him.

"Zel, we are very disappointed. When we invited you into our household to train our daughter, Rinetta, we did not expect you to steal from us."

Zel didn't say anything, just continued to make small sounds of distress, her trio of tails swishing in agitation. Rinetta, who indeed appeared to be Forsythia's daughter, looked distraught. She was little more than a child, maybe thirteen, yet she carried herself like she was accustomed to responsibility. She glanced from her mother to the Lynna like she wanted to say something. But whatever she'd been about to interject was lost as she pressed her lips together until the pink of them disappeared.

Interesting, Lando thought. He, however, had more urgent issues.

"Exalted, it seems you have a domestic dispute on your hands," he said. Every set of eyes in the room turned to him. "Perhaps it would be a good time for me to leave? Give you the privacy that such a delicate situation dictates."

"On the contrary, Calrissian. The sentence for attempted theft of a royal artifact is a simple one. The betrayer will be removed to the deepest, darkest hole of our dungeon, as befits her crime. And as the queen, it is our job to execute the laws of this land, even if it pains us to do so." The guards moved swiftly, each taking one of Zel's arms and dragging her out the door.

She had no overcoat, and Lando figured her thick fur, which had shaded to purple at the mention of the queen's dungeon, was most likely protection enough against the frigid Hynestian winds.

The bounty hunter saluted Forsythia and departed. Once the hunter was gone, Forsythia gestured, and one of her guards laid a thick blue pelt of gherlian fur across the table. She then made herself comfortable by propping one hip on the edge of the table.

"Lando Calrissian, do you know what the punishment is for those who smuggle contraband onto our planet?" Forsythia asked.

Lando grinned. "Exalted, I'm a legitimate businessman. An entrepreneur. What use would I have for such information?"

"Calrissian. Please. You'll find this goes much easier if we're honest with each other," she said. At some unspoken signal, one of the guards stepped closer, blaster pointed at Lando in an obviously threatening manner.

"Ah, well, I am not familiar with the punishment for smuggling on Hynestia, but I am getting the feeling that it isn't cake and a party," Lando quipped.

"Death is the punishment, Calrissian. Death by the Gran Kovali."

"Is that some kind of torture device?" Lando asked.

"It is the oldest living kova, a fierce reptile that lives

in the caves under our planet. We have heard that death by kova is particularly painful," Forsythia said, her tone mild, as if she were discussing the weather and not Lando's end.

"Oh, well, that doesn't sound very inviting," Lando said.

"You are going to find out, Calrissian. Purple glandis flower juice is illegal on Hynestia, and the bartender here was kind enough to confess that he got the juice from you, and thus your life is forfeit," Forsythia said with a note of finality. She stood to go, and Lando began to protest as the guard forced him to his feet.

"Exalted, please, perhaps there is something I could do—"

"Exalted Mother, perhaps he could be of assistance," came a small voice.

Everyone froze and turned to the girl, Rinetta. Her pale eyes watched Lando in a way that made him uncomfortable, but anything would be preferable to being eaten by a giant cave monster.

"Rinetta, we do not believe that Lando Calrissian can be trusted. It is best to have swift closure," Forsythia said, laying a gentle hand on her daughter's shoulder.

"Of course he can't, Exalted Mother. But you've already said that the Solstice Globe is too troublesome, the way someone is always trying to steal it." The girl looked at Lando, and he had the feeling that he was being sized up for a fleecing. It was like sitting in a high-stakes Sabacc game and holding nothing but garbage cards.

"Calrissian is a smuggler," the girl continued. "Have him take the orb to the Empire for us. If he fails in his mission or betrays us, we simply notify the Empire that he's stolen their tribute, and it becomes their problem."

Forsythia stilled, and suddenly Lando was less certain that the giant cave monster wasn't a better option.

"Rinetta, that is a brilliant idea." Forsythia turned back to Lando, and the smile on her face chilled Lando in a way not even the icy winds of Hynestia could. "It seems, Lando Calrissian, that you are to be spared. But first you must accomplish a small task for us."

"Worst luck," Lando muttered under his breath.

Rinetta stood back and tried to look haughty as the Royal Guard locked Zel Gris in the dungeon. Princesses in stories were always looking haughty, and Rinetta took that to be an expression somewhere between disdain and feigned interest. She tried her best to adopt such an expression now, but she mostly felt like she looked angry.

The Hynestian dungeon wasn't particularly awful, not like Rinetta had imagined. It was hewn out of rock and delightfully warm. Underground hot springs kept the caverns of Hynestia at a comfortable temperature, and the royal dungeon was no different. The cells were outlined in rough circles, and all of them were empty save for the one that housed Zel. It made Rinetta sad to see her friend in such a predicament, but she kept all her worry off her face. If Queen Forsythia knew what was going on, she would lock Rinetta in her rooms, and then the entire plan would be in shambles. At least for right now there was still a chance they could succeed.

Twyla, the head of the Royal Guard, locked the gate and nodded to Rinetta. "The prisoner is secured, Exalted."

"Leave us," Rinetta commanded, crossing her arms and sniffing. Twyla executed a complicated salute and left the dungeon, the rest of the guards trailing behind her. Rinetta waited until she heard the heavy clank of the security door before she moved toward the cell holding her tutor.

"Zel! I am so sorry! I didn't mean to be late. But why didn't you run away?" Rinetta asked.

Zel yowled in distress. Even though the cell was large it had been built for humans, and the Lynna was much bigger. Zel looked cramped and miserable. "I tried! I didn't have enough credits to book passage. I thought I could win some more in Sabacc, but that Calrissian cheats."

Rinetta sighed. "Did you at least send a message to your clan? Was it the Solstice Globe?"

Zel nodded, and her fur slowly shifted from gray to bright pink. "Yesssss! The elders have said that we can save everyone if we return it to its rightful place. But there isn't much time. There have been earthquakes, and the land grows colder in each passing moment. We must get it back to where it belongs."

Rinetta nodded. "Let me get you out of here."

Zel shook her head, her ears perking up as she

listened to some far-off noise. "No, there is no time. You heard the queen. She is going to use the globe as payment to the Empire. Once they have it there won't be any way for my people to get it back. You must steal it from Calrissian and take it to Livno III. Please. Before it's too late."

Rinetta took a step back. "Me? How am I supposed to do that?"

Zel purred and her tails swished. "You're clever, Princess Rinetta. You will figure something out. Remember the time you managed to trick Dobra into giving you two desserts? You can do this."

Rinetta sighed and leaned against the wall opposite Zel's cell. "This is all my fault. If I'd only managed to get to the cantina before that stupid bounty hunter I would've been able to warn you."

Zel shook her head. "There's no use in worrying about things like that now. We have to think about the best plan for the moment, not wish about the past."

"So that means stealing the Solstice Globe from Lando Calrissian," Rinetta said.

Zel sighed. "My dear princess, what have I taught you about strategy and critical thinking?"

Rinetta gnawed on her lower lip. Most of her courses with Zel had been about the great failures of battles throughout the galaxy and how a little rational thought could solve most issues before they became real problems. "Take my time and develop a course of action."

"Correct," Zel said with a purr. Even in a cell, she was still Rinetta's teacher. "And how do we do that?"

"State the problem, look at the relevant resources, exploit those resources to the best of our ability," Rinetta murmured, her mind working through the details. "I could steal the Solstice Globe, but then I would need a way to get it to Livno III. But Lando Calrissian has both a ship and the Solstice Globe, so my best course of action is to get Lando to take the orb back to Livno III."

Zel nodded, her fur shading to a deep blue that Rinetta knew meant her teacher was pleased. "Lando Calrissian is the tool you must exploit. You must discover a way to get him to help you. But it won't be easy."

Rinetta reached through the cell to grasp Zel's paw. "Okay, you're right. I'll figure out a way to make Calrissian take me to Livno. And when I get back, I'm getting you off of Hynestia and back home."

Zel nodded in agreement. "The necklace I gave you has very special properties." A few weeks earlier Zel had given Rinetta a necklace, a pretty purple stone hanging on a delicate silver chain. Rinetta had worn it every day since. The comforting weight of the stone pressed against her chest. "That is rare, ancient technology from my home planet. There is nothing else in the galaxy like it. The necklace will help you hide in plain view. Take it along with you and use it as necessary. Be careful, Princess Rinetta."

"Always," said Rinetta. She hoped she sounded brave.

She *felt* terrified. How in the name of the Gran Kovali was she supposed to convince a smuggler like Lando Calrissian to help her return a priceless artifact to a planet at the edge of the galaxy?

CHAPTER 5

Lando returned to the *Falcon* to find his navigator, L3-37, in a snit.

"Where have you been?" she demanded as he walked up the boarding ramp to the ship's interior. L3 pressed a button to raise the ramp and followed Lando as he made his way through the *Falcon*. "The yardmaster came by three separate times demanding payment for the docking and the fuel and you weren't here. I have things to do, you know, besides running interference on your debts."

Lando snorted. "What kind of pressing engagements do you have?"

L3 ignored the dig and drew herself up to her full height. She hadn't built a body to be talked down to by scruffy bandersnoots like Lando, even if he was her ship's captain. "That's not the point."

"What *is* the point, Elthree?"

L3 hummed in irritation. "The yardmaster was ready

to put a restraining bolt on me and take the *Falcon* as payment. That's the point. I hope you managed to at least make enough to cover our fuel. And we're out of cargo space. I filled up all of the secondary cargo space with your gherlian furs. They're bulkier than you described."

"Well, not that you care, but I ran into a bit of trouble." Lando sighed, dropping a bag that clacked as it hit the deck. A few creds spilled out. "But this should cover the yardmaster's debt."

"Define *trouble*," L3 said, her tone sharp. Unlike Lando, L3 didn't believe in luck. Or risk. Or Sabacc. She believed in rational decisions and hard-coded coordinates. It was why she was such a great navigator: she didn't leave things to chance. Mostly because that was how her data processor worked. But it was also what made her such an excellent first mate, especially with a captain like Lando. Nothing he ever came up with met her idea of reasonable. He was always barely two steps ahead of trouble, and he was a magnet for any and all kinds of misfortune. That was one of the reasons she enjoyed traveling with him. L3 had never met a human so prone to mishap.

Most of it was of his own doing.

Lando moved through the *Falcon* down to the galley, where he collapsed in one of the white chairs L3 had spent the afternoon polishing. She couldn't help it.

Lando had been gone long enough that she'd started to worry, and when she worried she cleaned. It wasn't that she liked cleaning; it was just that it was something to do.

"How would you feel about a trip out to the Guagenian sector?" Lando asked.

"That's the opposite way from Neral's moon and Cantonica. I thought you were going to pay off your debts before you were supposed to meet your buyer in Canto Bight?" L3 said. She crossed her metal arms, the whirring noise echoing slightly in the sudden quiet. "And you still haven't told me about this bit of trouble you ran into."

"That's because it's less trouble and more of an opportunity," Lando said.

L3 harrumphed. "Your 'opportunities' tend to be more effort than they're worth."

A clanging sound came from the entryway to the ship, and Lando stood slowly, stretching with a yawn. "Why don't you get that? If it's the yardmaster, his payment is in that bag I dropped back in the hold. I am going to get something to eat."

L3 made her way back to the boarding ramp. "Why is it that you always disappear when problems come knocking?" she muttered. Not for the first time, she considered walking off the *Falcon* and trying her luck as an independent droid. After all, she'd managed to build herself a body when her old one no longer served its purpose.

But she didn't know what she'd do, not really. And Lando wasn't the worst human she'd met. At least he treated her like a sentient being instead of a thing. And he did always notice when she was irritated. Even if he ignored it.

The clanging was still coming from the entryway to the cargo deck, and L3 figured the yardmaster had come once more to collect his debt. But when she lowered the boarding ramp, it wasn't the yardmaster, a grizzled human with pale skin and facial hair, who waited for her. Instead, it was a trio of humans dressed all in green, the color of the Hynestian Royal Guard.

It looked like Lando's trouble had found the *Falcon* after all.

"This cargo needs to be moved onto your ship," one of the humans said, pushing a large hovercrate forward. The other two humans stood far from the crate, as though they were afraid of it. They kept looking left and right, hands on their blasters, their posture stiff. Just what were they smuggling this time?

"You can place it right there," L3 said, pointing to the empty space in the cargo hold. If they were to tap any of the panels, dozens of gherlian furs would come spilling out, thousands of credits' worth of cargo and none of it the least bit legal. The trader who'd given them to Lando had said they shouldn't stick around long after the delivery, since the missing tribute to the Empire would be big news. But that was before Lando decided to take his chances at the Sabacc table and had whittled their fuel budget down to scraps. They'd been on Hynestia two days longer than planned, and if they didn't leave soon they would miss their rendezvous with the art dealer who had their relic. A relic that a very eager buyer on Canto Bight had promised a ridiculous number of credits for. Enough money that Lando could finally live his life as a sportsman, as he so often referred to his imagined life of leisure.

But that was only if they were able to make it to the meeting in time. And before they got there, they had to swing by Neral's moon and pay off Ne'eda Frip before she sent her henchmen, the Stalwarts, after them. They had a tight time schedule to meet, and from the looks of whatever was being delivered by the Hynestian Royal Guard, that wasn't going to happen.

One of the guards, a woman with pale skin and fiery red hair, turned to L3. "Make sure Calrissian knows that we have a tracker on that cargo. If he betrays the queen, we will find him and he will end up in service to the Gran Kovali."

"What is that, some kind of political office?"

The guard smiled. "One could say that." She turned and left without another word, and the low hum of concern that L3 had been ignoring blossomed into full-fledged alarm.

Once the crate was secured to the deck, L3 fidgeted with the controls and locked it so it wouldn't shift during takeoff. She eyed the crate, scanning it to see if there was any way to discern the contents. The crate was made of a heavy composite material she didn't recognize, but it set off all her sensors as being very, very expensive.

Whatever the crate contained, transporting it was undoubtedly a bad idea.

A thunk came from behind L3, and she turned around. It was an odd sound, like something heavy landing in the cargo area.

L3 walked over to the ramp and glanced down and then looked around at the cargo area.

Nothing. Strange.

She pushed the button to raise the boarding ramp and went back to studying the cargo container.

It wasn't until Lando returned, a half-eaten namba patty in his hand, that L3 let herself express the alarm humming through her circuits.

"Lando. What's in this crate?"

Lando shrugged. "No clue," he said, mouth full.

L3 pointed to the crate. "You just let the Hynestian Royal Guard load a heavily shielded crate onto the *Falcon*, and you don't know what's in it? Lando, this is reckless, and I'm not about to end up working on some gherlian farm because you've gone and gotten yourself killed."

"Baby, when have I ever let you down?" Lando asked, walking a slow circle around the crate.

"Well, there was that time on Gonda with the Sabacc game where you almost lost me to a Hutt on that awful bet, and that other time on Tatooine when you nearly lost the ship—"

"Okay, okay, point taken. But this isn't one of those times. And I don't know what's in the crate only because I haven't opened it yet. Queen Forsythia refused to say what it was, exactly. It's called the Solstice Globe. She just told me that it was a 'valuable energy source.' And anyway, I didn't have much of a choice. It was get this to a dealer in the outer reaches of the Guagenian Star Sea or get fed to some cave monster the Hynestians keep. So it looks like we're going to take a little detour."

"That is not a little detour. That is in the opposite direction," L3 said. "And there's a tracker on the crate."

"You can disarm it, right?"

L3 snorted. Well, she tried to snort. It sounded weird when she did it, but judging from the expression on Lando's face it was close enough to the real thing. "That tracker is top of the line. It can only be disarmed by the other half of the coding key."

Lando frowned. "So that's a no?"

"That is most definitely a no."

Lando waved his hand in dismissal. "Look, relax. We'll figure it out on the way. In fact, we can swing by and make the meet-up with our art dealer friend and then swing back around to the Guagenian sector and deliver this thing. It's not like Forsythia will care, as long as we get it to the dealer before Hynestia's payment to the Empire comes due."

L3 couldn't stop scanning the crate, because the more she did, the less certain she felt. "Maybe we should drop this out of the airlock once we hit deep space."

Lando laughed and patted L3 on the shoulder. "Don't worry, it'll be fine. Now, let's get off of this frozen rock before Queen Forsythia changes her mind and feeds me to her cave monster just because she's bored."

L3 shook her head and began plotting the flight path. "Why are people always trying to feed you to their pet monsters?"

Rinetta hid behind a stack of empty fuel cells and clutched her necklace firmly as she watched the Royal Guard load the crate carrying the Solstice Globe onto a blue-and-white ship. They didn't notice her, but she wasn't quite sure whether that was because of the necklace or because they weren't paying attention. Was she already too late? It seemed like she was always a few moments behind. Like with poor Zel. If Rinetta's plan had worked, she would've been in the cantina to help her tutor escape the bounty hunter. But instead she'd been forced to take Zel to the dungeon like she was some sort of criminal. And now there Rinetta was, stuck trying to figure out a way onto some old ship.

Most knew better than to cross Queen Forsythia. And those who didn't never got the chance to attempt it again. Rinetta wondered if she was making a huge mistake. What would her mother do when she found out?

Rinetta watched the Royal Guard leave and sighed.

She had so many misgivings about trying to convince Calrissian to help her. Smugglers never did anything altruistic and it would be difficult to trick him. She'd seen him in the cantina and knew from one look at him that he was shrewd. Crafty. The kind of person who knew how to get himself out of a scrape. Rinetta was smart, but she wasn't all that clever. It would be difficult to outwit someone like Lando Calrissian.

But she had to try.

She waited until the guards left before she sprinted across the empty yard. Once, Hynestia's landing yard had been filled with ships coming from every direction in the galaxy, all there to buy gherlian in every shade of the rainbow. But now there were only a few pathetic vessels, most of them from refugees or smugglers. Hynestia was no longer the trade port it had once been, and it was all the Empire's fault. The queen thought the deal she'd made had been a good one, one that kept the Emperor's stormtroopers off the surface of their planet. But anyone could see that they'd opted for a slow decay instead of outright conquest. Even if Rinetta did somehow become queen, she would rule over an empty husk of a planet, the best part of their resources sucked dry by the ever-expanding Empire.

Rinetta was not about to let that happen.

She hurdled an empty fuel canister and skidded to a stop behind one of the giant struts of the ship's landing gear. Rinetta took a deep breath and let it out before she edged to the ramp of the ship and peered into the cargo hold.

Empty. Perfect.

Rinetta crouched as she tiptoed up the ramp. She was almost inside, her goal the shipping container carrying the Solstice Globe, when she spied the droid. The thing was oddly shaped, an astromech's dome perched on a messily wired body. There was no way around it, though, the droid stood in between Rinetta and her goal.

Without a second thought Rinetta tapped a button on her ankle and jumped, twisting her body around in what would have been an impressive handspring if the boots hadn't been engaged. The boots were equipped with heavy-duty magnets, and once the bottoms faced the top of the ship, they pulled Rinetta into the air, the only sound a soft thump as they fastened to the ceiling.

Rinetta tucked her body back toward her feet, wrapping her arms around her knees so she was a lump on the roof of the cargo hold. And then, before the droid could turn fully around, she clutched the necklace Zel had given her, engaging its strange and unusual power once more. As long as she remained still, she was invisible.

The droid turned around, looking for the source of the thump. Rinetta held her breath, worried that even the soft rise and fall of her chest might tip off the droid. But it seemed to shrug, of all things, and went back to whatever duties it had been attending to. It knocked three times on a panel, opening it and shifting around something that Rinetta couldn't see from her vantage point. But Rinetta didn't need to see the cargo to know what a hidden panel meant. Lando Calrissian was a smuggler after all.

Rinetta let out her breath and waited until the droid and Lando had come and gone before she released her necklace and disengaged her boots. She quickly made her way to the container and disarmed the tracking beacon on the crate. Twyla used the same code to lock everything, and Rinetta had memorized it long before so she could have unfettered access to anything she chose. And Queen Forsythia had given Rinetta the other part of the code when she'd asked to take on more responsibility. So Rinetta had parts one and two to every code in the kingdom. Good thing, too. Otherwise, they'd never make it to Livno

Footsteps echoed through the adjacent corridor, and Rinetta grabbed her necklace and pressed against the wall as Lando Calrissian walked back through the cargo bay, whistling a merry tune as he went. He didn't seem to see her, and Rinetta relaxed as she spotted the blaster hanging low in the holster on his hip.

She had an idea.

While Lando fidgeted with his hair in a mirror attached to a wall near the shipping container, she tiptoed up behind him and carefully tugged the blaster loose. Rinetta half expected him to feel the weight lifting out of his holster, but he was so intent on his grooming that he never even noticed.

Amazing.

Rinetta tucked herself back into the space between the shipping container and the wall and watched as Lando grinned at his reflection in the mirror before giving himself a saucy wink. "You're doing great, baby," he said before strutting toward what Rinetta figured must be the cockpit.

Rinetta hefted the blaster and smiled. Lando Calrissian thought he was going to deliver the Solstice Globe to an agent of the Empire for Queen Forsythia, but Rinetta had other plans. The Solstice Globe was going back where it belonged.

And Lando Calrissian was going to be the one to deliver it, whether he wanted to or not.

After L3-37 had charted a course and taken them into a hyperspace jump, Lando decided that a nap was in order. It had been a very long day, and the jump to Neral's moon would take most of the night. So Lando changed into pajamas and got some sleep while L3, who didn't really need rest, flew the ship.

Lando woke feeling refreshed and recharged. Naps were always a great way to reset. Hynestia had been a brief hiccup, but everything was back under control. Lando changed into what he thought of as his flying outfit—blue shirt, gray pants, and his favorite lemon-yellow cape—and returned to the cockpit. He sat down at the yoke, relaxing into the comfortable herdon leather of his chair while L3 ignored him.

Perfect.

"You know, after we're done on Neral's moon we should think about getting over to the Fimster Quadrant. We should get the ship cleaned again. It's starting to look a little dingy."

"Maybe you should be thinking about what we're going to tell Ne'eda Frip when she asks where her purple glandis flower juice is."

"Ne'eda isn't going to be a problem, Elthree. We've got more than enough credits to pay off our debt. And besides, we have a few dozen extra gherlian furs. We can bribe her with a couple of those. Trust me, if there's one thing women like, it's pretty things," Lando said with a wink.

L3 crossed her arms and looked at Lando with what he could only think of as her disapproving face. It wasn't so much an actual expression as the tilt of her dome. "What?" Lando asked.

"Have you considered that women are not a single species for you to make assumptions about? They are complex, and Ne'eda is just as likely to have her Stalwarts give you a thrashing for trying to cheat her as she is—did you hear that?"

Lando turned his head to the side, listening. From somewhere in the ship came the sound of something scraping against the floor.

"Elthree, I told you we have to secure the containers before we jump to hyperspace. How long has that been rolling around the cargo hold? You know I hate when the floor gets scratched." Lando stood to walk back to the cargo bay when the door to the cockpit slid open. For a long moment he just stared, because there was no way he was seeing what he thought he was seeing.

The princess from Hynestia—Rinetta, her mother had called her—was standing in the doorway with a blaster pointed right at his chest. *His* blaster, of all things.

"Well, hello there," Lando said, grinning. He'd had blasters pointed at him before, but never by a girl of no more than thirteen, and never his own blaster. He was usually better at planning than that. In fact, how'd she even get it? He could've sworn it was on his hip. But a quick check provided nothing more than an empty holster. "Are you lost, sweetheart?"

"Can it, smuggler," the girl said, waving him back toward his seat with the blaster. "Sit back down."

Lando backed up carefully, and L3 swiveled around in her seat. She tilted her head toward Rinetta. "Friend of yours?" she asked Lando.

"Hardly," Rinetta said, her eyes locked on Lando, before turning to L3. "I need you to recalibrate the jump to take us to Livno III."

L3 made a wheezing noise that was her version of laughter. "No can do, bugaloo," she said.

"Listen, droid, I gave you an order, and you'd better do it," Rinetta said. Her bottom lip jutted out in defiance, and Lando relaxed into his chair just a bit. Was this whole thing the result of a royal temper tantrum?

"Who are you calling 'droid'? My name is Elthree,

and I am a navigator, thank you very much. Children these days are so rude, stowing away and pointing blasters at people," L3 muttered.

"Not now, Elthree," Lando whisper-yelled at his navigator. He turned back to Rinetta, twisting around in his chair. "I'm afraid Elthree pretty much does what she's told when she feels like it, if even then," Lando said.

The girl looked to Lando and then L3, her face contorted with surprise. "Why would you keep a droid around who doesn't listen?"

"Because of my amazing personality, obviously," L3 said. "And if you call me a droid one more time, I'm going to take that blaster and—"

"Whoa, whoa, Elthree, let me take care of this." Lando shrugged at Rinetta's look of disbelief. "She's a really good navigator. And please don't call her a droid like that. It's rude."

Rinetta shook herself, as though she'd just remembered she was holding a blaster. "Look, I don't care. We need to go to Livno and that's—"

A bump and slight shudder cut the girl off, and the streaky blue tunnel of hyperspace melted away into the inky blackness of deep space. Off in the distance glowed a bright green-and-pink moon, beckoning ships forward. A clearly marked asteroid field lay between the *Falcon* and the satellite.

"What is that? Where are we?" Rinetta asked, leaning

forward. Her grip on the blaster loosened, and Lando took his chance. He grabbed it, pushing the girl back into the jump seat at the same time. She landed in the chair with a soft *oof*, and Lando pointed the blaster at her.

"That is Neral's moon, the premier entertainment hub in the Corellian sector. Fashion, fame, fun—all of it can be found on Neral's moon."

L3 huffed. "You sound like an advertisement."

Lando gave L3 a withering look before turning back to Rinetta. "We have business here. And while I admire your sense of adventure, I'm afraid my good humor doesn't extend to being on the wrong side of a blaster, especially when it's held by a child."

The girl's brown cheeks took on a ruddy hue. "I'm not a child, I'm thirteen!"

Lando grinned and shook his head. "With a mother like yours you'd think you would be more sensible. Anyway, Elthree, do we have some sort of restraint for the girl? I'd rather not have to worry about being attacked by a Hynestian princess while I'm trying to navigate an asteroid field."

"How would I know?" L3 barked, and Lando shook his head and holstered his weapon.

"Why don't you take her back to the lounge and find some way to secure her?" Lando asked, trying a different tactic.

"I'm the copilot, not the warden," L3 said, not bothering to move a centimeter.

Lando sighed deeply. "Fine," he said.

The *Falcon* shuddered and lurched, and a scraping sound echoed throughout the cockpit. "Gah, my ship," Lando said, sitting back down in his chair and scanning the readout for any errors.

"Stray asteroid," L3 said.

"Find us the way through this mess," Lando snapped, his usual good cheer falling away. "I just had the *Falcon* repainted, and I am not about to arrive looking scruffy."

Lando turned back to Rinetta to make sure she was still in the jump seat, but she hadn't moved. She sat with arms crossed, mouth tight. Lando realized she was fighting back tears, and he sighed. "Look, kiddo, it was an impressive plan, hijacking your mom's cargo. Were you planning on selling it to buy candy or something?"

The girl scowled at Lando. "Candy? Are you serious? No, I had something I needed to do. I made a promise, and I have a responsibility to keep it."

"And what kind of promise requires you to sneak aboard my ship and point a blaster at my head?" Lando kept one hand on the yoke and one eye on the girl. He was giving himself a crick in his neck, but maybe he could find some time to get a massage while on Neral's moon. He was going to need it.

Princess Rinetta didn't say anything, just clamped

her lips shut again and crossed her arms tighter. Lando shrugged.

"Fine, keep your secrets," he said. He stood and pointed the blaster at Rinetta again. "Let's take a walk."

The girl stood and walked back toward the lounge, and Lando followed, the blaster pointed at the small of her back. He had no intention of shooting a Hynestian royal princess. That would be way more trouble than she was worth, but she didn't know that.

"Hello, we're in the middle of an asteroid field. Is anyone going to help me fly this thing?" L3 called down the hallway. Lando ignored her. He had more pressing matters to deal with.

Once they were in the lounge, Lando gestured to the settee in the middle of the room. "Sit," he commanded. The girl sank like a chunk of carbonite, her expression just as stony. Lando didn't bother asking her again why she was on the *Millennium Falcon*. He knew a game face when he saw one.

Lando looked through a cupboard and found a set of brightly colored scarves left behind from his fancy phase—he really did look excellent with a scarf tied just so around his neck—and used them to tie Rinetta's hands behind her back and then to a crossbar secured to the floor.

"Stay," Lando said, and then made his way back to the cockpit.

"So, what are we going to do about the kid?" L3 asked once Lando had settled back into the captain's seat.

"Nothing."

She turned toward him, her dome cocked slightly to the side. "Nothing?"

"My bet is her mom is already on her way here. No way Forsythia isn't going to have some sort of tracker on her kid, not a kid like that. We conduct our business as quickly as possible and get Forsythia's crate to her buyer before the queen of Hynestia figures out we have a ship full of stolen gherlian furs. She finds out we have those, we might as well kiss our payday good-bye."

L3 shook her head. "Have you considered that maybe this plan is getting more complicated by the minute? Maybe we should cut our losses."

"Nonsense, baby," Lando said, grinning at L3. "We're only getting started."

Lando set the *Falcon* down gently in the landing bay of Neral's moon. Despite the Hynestian princess pointing a blaster at him—his own blaster, for that matter—he felt good. Happy. Lucky. He might have a princess tied up in his lounge, but he had a ship full of gherlian furs, and he was about to pay off one of his outstanding debts. Normally, paying someone back would put Lando in a terrible funk, but not this time.

This time, he was coming out ahead. He was sure of it.

Neral's moon was the kind of place where one could find anything to do. Podracing? Definitely. Unta fish juggling? Sure, why not. Sabacc? Of course. If it was fun and people were paying money to do it, you could find it on Neral's moon.

Not that Ne'eda, the moon's owner, was known for fun. She was better known for thrashing folks who wronged her. But Lando had always done well by Ne'eda, and in return Ne'eda had never sent her Stalwarts, the crew that kept order on Neral's moon, after him.

That had all changed a little while before, when Lando had fled the moon without paying his debt after a particularly terrible round of Sabacc. To be fair, it was mostly because he hadn't cheated. If he'd been cheating he would've won more hands. And that was the time he'd wagered L3-37. Well, one of them. The truth was, the *Falcon* didn't run so hot without L3. The ship needed her, and L3 had kept Lando from crashing into a moon or a planet while in hyperspace more than once. He couldn't very well lose her.

So he'd skipped out on his debt. And Ne'eda had been after him ever since. Her last message had been simple and straight to the point: he would give her what he owed or she would send her Stalwarts to end him. Painfully.

Lando was smart. He didn't need to be told twice.

So there he was once again, on Neral's moon, hoping to make things right with Ne'eda. Clear his debts, so to speak. He carried with him a small swatch of gherlian fur tucked inside the lining of his cape, a hidden pocket he'd been delighted to find after buying the lemon-yellow garment, and whistled as he walked up to the tower. Neral's moon was watery, covered in beautiful multihued canals. Bioluminescent creatures called klinnet glimmered in the water, casting enough light to see by. Their glow was even visible from space. The first time Lando had visited the moon he'd been young, and he'd spent a ridiculously long time staring at the water, trying to figure out what caused the radiance. It wasn't until one of the creatures had swum to the surface and splashed him with a large dorsal fin that he'd moved. His embarrassment had quickly surpassed his curiosity.

This time he took in the sight with appreciation but never slowed his steps. He had to find Ne'eda before her Stalwarts found him.

The automatic doors of Ne'eda's Tower, the largest gaming parlor on the moon, slid open with a pressurized hiss, and Lando stood inside the entryway for a moment to get his bearings. Creatures of all kinds milled about, from humans eating frozen joral cream to Zygerrians laughing as they played hologames. Most everyone had dressed to impress, the women wearing gowns that sparkled and draped beautifully and the men boasting only the finest suits. Lando spotted a couple of bounty hunters milling about in their distinctive Tantel armor and skirted them easily by keeping a good chunk of the crowd around him at all times. It wasn't that he thought there was a bounty on his head, but one could never be too sure.

Either way, Lando felt a particular lightness in his chest. He really did like Neral's moon, especially Ne'eda's gaming parlor. It catered to the highest of high-end clients, and Lando was delighted to note that he fit right in.

Lando spotted the Sabacc tables and paused. Now that he thought about it, maybe he could squeeze in a game or two before he found Ne'eda.

He'd gone only a few steps toward the Sabacc tables before a large Wookiee stepped into his path, howling something in Shyriiwook.

"Oh, hello, friend. I don't suppose you know where I can find Ne'eda?" Lando asked.

The Wookiee responded by grabbing Lando's upper arm and fairly lifting him off his feet as he dragged him toward a turbolift located behind a bank of large, leafy potted ferns.

"Friend, I assure you this isn't necessary," Lando said, but the furry creature didn't listen. Lando could either run along on tiptoes or be dragged, so he ran. He didn't even want to consider what the rough grip was doing to the fine cloth of his cape.

Lando smiled and waved at people who stared as the Wookiee dragged him through the lobby and to the turbolift.

Once inside, the Wookiee released Lando. He smoothed his clothes. "I genuinely hope this isn't wrinkled," Lando muttered, straightening his shirt and adjusting his cape. Honestly, while he understood the need for a businesswoman like Ne'eda to have a certain kind of staff to ensure her interests were served, he did not like being treated like some common criminal.

There was nothing common about Lando Calrissian.

Lando felt a bit queasy as the turbolift sped to the top of the tower, but by the time the door opened, he'd plastered his characteristic smile back on his face.

"Ne'eda," Lando said, hands held out to show he was unarmed. As if the Wookiee would've brought him to Ne'eda's den without checking him for weapons. "It is a delight to see you again. You are looking as beautiful as ever. Did you just molt?"

The penthouse of Ne'eda's Tower belonged to the gaming parlor's namesake. There was very little space for the Wookiee and Lando, though; a huge tank took up nearly the entire floor. Inside the tank sat Ne'eda, head of the Stalwarts and the undisputed ruler of the moon.

Ne'eda growled underwater when she saw Lando. He wasn't sure what kind of creature Ne'eda was, but she looked fierce. She was bright purple and had two arms and a powerful tail lined with vicious-looking spikes. On either side of her neck were large gills, and fan-shaped fins protruded from her head where her ears would be if she were human. The one time Lando had seen her leave the tank, it had been to swallow a man whole. The human had owed her money, and when he couldn't pay she'd climbed out of her tank,

dragged herself across the floor with her clawed hands, unhinged her jaw, and swallowed him down.

It was a fate Lando very much wanted to avoid. In fact, if he could avoid being eaten altogether, that would be swell.

His luck held, because Ne'eda didn't climb out of her tank. Instead she leaned back, her facial fins flaring this way and that. A series of gurgles followed, bubbles floating to the top of the brackish water.

"She says that you are a terrible liar and that you owe her four thousand credits," said a droid standing next to the tank. The protocol droid was on the small side, but with Ne'eda looming over him in her tank he felt much more imposing.

"I am not lying, Ne'eda, you look absolutely vibrant. Just completely rejuvenated since the last time I saw you, and I have returned to settle my debt. Although, I'm pretty sure it was only two thousand credits the last time we spoke."

Ne'eda burbled, and the droid translated. "That was before interest. You owe four thousand credits now."

"Ah, of course," Lando said. "Well, I am afraid I don't have enough credits, then, and I am fresh out of purple glandis flower juice, but I have brought you something even better." Lando pulled out the scrap of gherlian fur dramatically, holding it up so it could catch the light. He waited for the sounds of exclamation and astonishment that were sure to follow.

He was sorely disappointed.

Ne'eda gurgled, swimming to the left and to the right in her tank as she tried to get a better look at what Lando held.

"She wants to know what it is," the droid said, voice deadpan. Ne'eda's droid reminded Lando of just how terribly behaved L3 was. Maybe he'd ask Ne'eda for some tips once they settled their business. It would be nice if L3 just did what she was asked instead of arguing all the time.

"What?" Lando finally asked after he realized his mind had wandered.

More sounds from Ne'eda. More droid translations. "The thing you're holding. She asked if it was food, because it doesn't smell like food."

"What, this? No, it's not food. But I am impressed you can smell food even from inside the tank. Seriously, very impressed. No, this is gherlian fur. A single pelt can be worth several thousand credits. Just this piece alone is worth a hundred credits."

Ne'eda shook her head. "She doesn't care for the skins of dead creatures," the droid said.

"What, but it's not a dead creature," Lando sputtered. "It's a very particular kind of lichen that grows only on Hynestia. The Empire has started to demand the entirety of the planet's production, which is why it's so valuable," Lando said. For the first time, a bit of worry began to creep in. He hadn't actually thought

Ne'eda would refuse the gherlian furs. After all, she could sell them for a handsome profit.

"So the furs are controlled by the Empire. Meaning that reselling them will immediately set off any number of alerts," the droid said, once again interpreting Ne'eda's burblings. "Do you take me for a fool, Calrissian?"

"Now, Ne'eda, I think there must be some kind of misunderstanding," Lando said as the Wookiee grabbed him once more.

"Mistress Ne'eda is not confused," the droid translated in its flat voice. "The deal was for you to deliver thirty barrels of purple glandis flower juice or pay the credits you owe. Otherwise, your life would be forfeit. You have brought no credits, there is no glandis flower juice, and my mistress is hungry." The droid stepped back, and Ne'eda hauled herself out of the tank, flipping over the side and landing on the floor with a heavy splat.

The Wookiee pushed Lando toward Ne'eda. Her mouth opened unnaturally wide. Lando tried to fight his way free, but the Wookiee was too strong, and there was nowhere for him to go.

It looked as though maybe his luck had actually run out.

Rinetta fumed as she watched L3-37 bustle about the *Millennium Falcon*. The droid was attending to business of her own and paid no attention to Rinetta, who had waited until Lando left before sliding a portable plasma blade down her sleeve and cutting away at the ridiculous scarves that bound her hands. Only a dandy like Calrissian would secure a renegade princess with scarves, of all things.

Once she was free, Rinetta sat for a moment and considered her options. She needed Lando to help her get the Solstice Globe to Livno III. She'd watched as he and his droid had piloted the *Falcon* through the asteroid field, and it was clear that flying such a ship was too much for her to handle by herself. If she could avoid Lando Calrissian, Rinetta would, but she didn't know how to fly a ship and the droid seemed to be strictly about navigation. So whatever happened next would require Lando.

Rinetta tilted her head and listened for a moment for the plodding steps of the droid. When none were forthcoming, she stood and made her way to the cargo bay and the boarding ramp off the ship. Rinetta had never been to Neral's moon, even though she'd heard about it from various tutors during galaxy mapping courses. Once Neral had been a prosperous planet, rich in natural resources. But a series of volcanic eruptions had violently destabilized the core, and the planet had exploded, leaving behind nothing but an asteroid field and a moon. Rinetta had already seen the asteroid field. Now she wanted to see the moon.

Rinetta fairly skipped down the ramp, her excitement was so great. Sure, her plan had failed miserably. She hadn't been counting on Lando Calrissian being so clever and snatching the blaster out of her hands. Nor had she counted on meeting a droid that didn't do what it was told. But even though she hadn't accomplished her mission, Rinetta was still having an adventure. For what seemed like her entire life, she'd dreamed about traveling to other planets the way her ancestors had. Once upon a time, Hynestians had been known throughout the galaxy as great travelers and sometimes conquerors. Now they were known as lichen farmers. Rinetta knew which one she would choose if she *had* a choice.

So for the moment, she would live her heart's desire: she would explore Neral's moon.

Rinetta easily made her way off the *Falcon* and into the docking bay. Instead of going straight to the gaming areas, Rinetta decided to wander a little. The docking bay was filled with ships of all kinds, even an Imperial frigate. Rinetta made the sign of ill luck at the ship, but not too obviously. She didn't want to draw attention to herself.

Rinetta walked between the ships, studying the makes and models. Lando's Corellian freighter looked out of place among the brand-new pleasure crafts, its circular shape distinct. Rinetta wondered if that bothered him. Lando seemed like the kind of man who cared very deeply about appearances. And sure, the *Falcon* was clean and sparkling, but it still wasn't a pleasure yacht. Was that something Rinetta could use to convince him to help her? After all, he was ridiculously flashy. His clothes were very expensive, and in her snooping around the ship she'd found no fewer than forty capes. Forty! Who in the galaxy needed that many capes?

Rinetta finished scoping out the other ships in the docking bay and made her way down a lighted path to the gaming areas. She'd only gotten a few steps outside of the building when she halted.

The canals were glowing.

Small, luminous creatures filled the water. Rinetta crept closer to see, sliding down a grassy incline. She made sure not to get her feet wet, since there was no knowing if the water was safe for humans. But she didn't have to get in to observe the life beneath the surface.

The creatures were small, no longer than her finger, and they had what looked like four tiny arms and very long webbed tails. As they moved they flashed at each other, but they were so small that the flashing took on a glimmering effect. The canals mostly glowed all the same color: pink or green, with the occasional purple. Rinetta didn't know what the colors meant, but they were beautiful.

"Klinnet," said someone behind her. Rinetta frowned.

"Klin-net?" Rinetta straightened and turned to see a food peddler watching her from up on the path. Rinetta's Basic was pretty good, but she didn't know that word. And she was pretty sure no one on Neral's moon spoke High Hynestian. Maybe the word was some kind of Basic slang term? "What's a klinnet?"

The woman smiled down at Rinetta. "The creatures in the canals. The colors are how they talk to each other."

"But why are they all the same color?" Rinetta wondered out loud.

"Klinnet that are flashing pink can only talk to other klinnet flashing pink. And green to green. They're like comlink channels," the woman said. "Would you like a bantha patty? They're good, and you can feed the klinnet with them."

"No, thank you, but I appreciate you telling me about the klinnet." Rinetta scrambled up the slope and back to the path. She didn't have time to sightsee right then, but one day she would.

Signs in Basic flashed everywhere, and Rinetta puzzled out two that urged her toward the podracing arena and the hologames. Rinetta wasn't sure where to go until she managed to translate a sign that seemed familiar: NE'EDA'S TOWER, THE PLACE TO GO FOR ALL KINDS OF FUN.

Lando and L3 had talked about Lando's debt to a Ne'eda, and Rinetta was willing to bet that was where he'd gone.

So she headed there, as well.

Rinetta couldn't help gawking as she walked. So many different kinds of people gathered on Neral's moon. Rinetta had met several different species while following her mother on official business, but she'd never seen so many crowded into a single place. It made her feel happy and welcome to walk among such a morass of life, as though she wasn't a princess with a great responsibility on her shoulders but just another girl out to have some fun.

At least until a hand snaked out and grabbed her arm. "Is that gherlian fur?"

Rinetta turned to find a small man grinning at her. His eyes were bright blue and his ears were a little pointed, but he looked mostly human.

"Yes, why?"

"I'll give you a thousand credits for that tunic." He held out a bag of coins that he shook in her direction. They clinked and jangled in a way that probably would have been appealing to most folks.

"No," she said, pulling her arm free and continuing toward the tower. Rinetta had no use for money. All she needed was Lando and his ship. If the man had offered to trade her Lando Calrissian's willing compliance, maybe she would've hesitated.

"Wait! I'll give you two thousand credits and this blaster!" the man yelled.

Rinetta slid to a stop. A blaster could be useful.

"Show me," Rinetta said. She didn't have much use for credits—as a princess, she mostly got everything she wanted—but maybe she'd gone about things the wrong way earlier. Threatening to shoot someone wasn't a very good tactic. Queen Forsythia said that negotiations should be opened in a way that made everyone believe they had a choice, and by threatening to shoot Lando she had definitely eliminated any pretense of giving him a chance to plead his case. Maybe if she offered to pay him he would be more willing to help her return the Solstice Globe to Livno III.

And if he refused, then she would threaten to shoot him.

The man pulled out a tiny holdout blaster, much

smaller than Lando's larger model and the perfect size for a princess to conceal under her dress—if Rinetta had been one to wear dresses. Still, it was a fair trade, and she needed the blaster more than she needed the gherlian fur tunic. Neral's moon was warm, and she'd begun sweating almost as soon as she'd left the *Millennium Falcon*.

"That's a fair trade," Rinetta said, and the man hopped a little in delight. She unbelted the gherlian fur tunic and removed it, leaving just her underdress, and the man grabbed it before throwing the blaster and bag at her and running off.

For a moment Rinetta worried that she'd gotten a raw deal, but when she opened the bag, all the money was there, as well as a half-eaten piece of some kind of weird purple fruit.

Rinetta fastened her belt, tucked the holdout blaster in her waistband, and made her way toward Ne'eda's Tower.

Lando Calrissian wouldn't know what hit him.

L3-37 paced in the cargo bay of the *Millennium Falcon*, worry sizzling across her circuits. There was something off about this cargo. She could feel it in her wires. Such a heavily shielded cargo container, and now the girl stowing away on the *Falcon*? There was trouble afoot. And somehow Lando wasn't to blame this time.

Well, as far as L3 knew. There was still a good chance this was all his fault. He was a smuggler, after all—when he wasn't cheating at Sabacc.

L3 looked at the container one last time before heading back up to the lounge, where Rinetta was tied up. But when she got there, the girl was nowhere to be found. All that was left was a set of singed scarves, most likely burned through with a pocket plasma cutter.

Well, looks like Lando is about to have some company, L3 thought. Served him right. He was always being a little too risky with their lives. Maybe the small human could startle some sense into him.

It would probably be a good time to do some maintenance checks on the *Millennium Falcon*. L3 had a feeling they would need to leave quickly.

She had just run through a systems check and was walking outside to check the exterior of the ship—they had run into a few asteroids, after all—when there was a pounding on the gangway to the *Falcon*. She made her way to the cargo deck, where a bounty hunter stood. Her blue skin and bright green hair left no mistaking who she was. The last time Lando had run afoul of the woman, L3 had almost ended up scrapped for parts. Jeskian Veldar worked for the most ruthless cartels in the galaxy, and her presence on Neral's moon couldn't mean anything good.

A green, snout-nosed Gamorrean and a couple of scruffy-looking humans stood behind her. A droid painted all black stood a little farther back in the docking bay. The droid turned toward L3 with a menacing air, and she realized that if she were organic she would have shivered. This crew was rougher than the lot who usually did business with Lando and his friends. Even Jeskian had a ragged look to her, the long scar bisecting the left side of her face giving her a menacing air. They looked like they would dismantle L3 for parts and never think twice about it.

They looked ruthless.

"Where's Calrissian?" the bounty hunter asked,

blaster unholstered and pointed right at L3. This was the second time in a very short while that someone had pointed a blaster at her, and she didn't care for it.

L3 beeped and answered in her most droid-like voice: "Captain Calrissian is currently taking in the sights of Neral's moon. I believe he was making his way to the observation tower." No one ever expected droids to do anything but answer questions directly, so L3 hoped it wouldn't occur to the bounty hunter that she was lying.

The bounty hunter stared at L3 for a long moment before holstering her weapon and walking back down the gangplank to the docking bay.

L3 waited until the bounty hunter had left before she walked to the cockpit and tried to get Lando on his comlink.

"Lando, do you hear me? Lando! There's a bounty hunter headed right for you!" There was no response, but there was a beep from somewhere behind L3.

She turned to find the black droid standing right behind her, his single optical sensor glowing red.

"Provide the coordinates to Lando Calrissian or face the consequences," the droid said. He had a blaster pointed right at L3's dome.

L3 raised her hands in surrender. "I do not know the coordinates to Lando Calrissian," she said, mimicking the droid's stilted speech. "I was instructed to warn him of any potential pursuit, but my *master*"—L3 spit the word out before she lost her nerve and gave away the act—"did not give me any further instructions except to say that he had gone to the observation tower and to raise him on his comlink as soon as possible."

The sentry droid didn't lower his blaster, and for a long moment L3 was afraid she was about to be repurposed.

But then the sentry droid stiffened and fell to the ground in a heap of limbs and circuits, humming a low tone. Smoke rose from his back, and if L3 could smell she was certain her nose would be filled with the stink of ozone and burning circuits.

A woman stood behind the sentry droid with a blaster in her hand. Her hair circled her head in a set of ornate braids, even though her clothing was more serviceable than decorative. But the way the woman carried herself and her features, so like those of the girl who had pointed a blaster at Lando and L3 earlier, erased all doubt as to her identity.

"Exalted," L3 said, knowing well enough when it was time to use her best manners.

"Yes, droid, we are Queen Forsythia," the woman said, not bothering to lower the blaster that was pointed right at L3. "Where is our daughter?"

CHAPTER 11

Lando needed a plan.

L3-37 was going on about something in his com-link, so he silenced the chirping in his ear. Whatever she needed, a new bottle of gear oil or whatever, would just have to wait until some other time. He had much bigger problems to deal with.

He glanced down Ne'eda's gaping maw at her six—no, seven!—rows of razor-sharp teeth and tried to think of something to say, something to promise that would save him from being dinner. Or breakfast. Whatever. He needed to focus.

"Ne'eda, I'm afraid I neglected to mention the other part of my offer!" Lando said, trying to wriggle from the Wookiee's grasp. "A valuable treasure deep from within the vault of Hynestia! Rarer than a crown jewel!"

Ne'eda hesitated, closing her mouth and leaning back in a way that clearly indicated she was interested. Lando kept talking.

"It is a thing of unspeakable beauty and power, and

I just happen to have it on the *Falcon*. Just send your droid and Wookiee along with me and I'll give it to them, and then we'll be square, okay?" His voice was a bit higher than normal, and he cleared his throat. "Ne'eda, trust me when I say I only want what's best for you and your enterprise. I miscalculated with the gherlian furs, not a problem. But this? This incredible . . . uh . . . device? This you will adore." Lando realized he still didn't know what the cargo he carried aboard his ship was or what it actually did. Just that it was valuable and important enough to cause a princess to stow away on the *Millennium Falcon*—which was, of course, concerning. Usually he was much better about knowing and working every angle, not just the most expedient ones.

Ne'eda burbled and moved back to her tank. She used the suction cups on her palms to lift herself into the murky water and, once there, gurgled something long and complex.

"Ne'eda is disappointed in your failure, but she is also intrigued by your tale of Hynestian royal plunder," the droid said. "So she will send you back to your ship with her Stalwart in order that he might ascertain what kind of treasure you might possess. And if you are lying, your life will be forfeit."

Lando sketched a bow. "More than fair enough."

"Of course it is," the droid said. "Mistress Ne'eda takes her business very seriously."

The Wookiee still had his heavy, furry hand on Lando's shoulder, and he turned the smuggler around and pushed him toward the turbolift, bellowing something unintelligible in Shyriiwook.

"Yes, yes, to the ship," Lando muttered, walking into the turbolift.

Once they entered and the doors closed, Lando began to consider his options. He had no intention of taking Ne'eda's Stalwart onto his ship. Even though he'd nearly been eaten, Lando figured he still had time to get Ne'eda her purple glandis flower juice. All he had to do was find a way to sell off the gherlian furs, drop off the Hynestian cargo, and make his way back to Coruscant to find someone willing to sell him forty barrels of purple glandis flower juice. He owed her thirty, but if he took her extra she would forgive him for what he was about to do to her Stalwart.

The turbolift doors opened to reveal a Quarren male, his facial tentacles waving in agitation. Behind him was a bounty hunter in blue-and-black armor with a sleek blue helmet.

"Halt. We are here for Calrissian," the bounty hunter said, his voice modulator echoing oddly.

"What, why? What did I do?" Lando demanded.

"Jeskian Veldar wants her money," the bounty hunter said.

Lando grimaced. "I told Jeskian I had a line on an

artifact I was going to bring her! Doesn't anyone have any kind of faith anymore?"

The Wookiee pushed Lando behind him and bleated something at the bounty hunter.

"I don't care what kind of debt he has to your mistress, I have a bounty to collect," the hunter said. The Quarren male ran off, smart enough to know he didn't want to be in the midst of an argument between a bounty hunter and a Wookiee. Lando wished he could make a similar escape.

Lando took a deep breath. Normally, he was adept at balancing his debts in such a way that they didn't inconvenience him, but that day was exceptionally bad. There was no way he could pay both Ne'eda and Jeskian. Not immediately.

Talk about a run of bad luck.

"Pssst."

Lando looked around at the sudden sound while the Wookiee and the bounty hunter continued to argue a meter away. The potted plant next to him rustled, and a brown face peeked through the foliage.

"Princess Rinetta," Lando said with a sigh. "Now is not a good time."

"If you take me to Livno, I will help you get out of this," she said.

Lando swallowed a bark of laughter. "Look, I genuinely appreciate the sentiment, but what can you do? You're just a child."

She set her jaw and shook her head. "Just trust me."

Rinetta pulled him backward into the branches of the potted plant.

"Stay still," she said in a low voice. "They can't see us as long as I use my necklace, but they can hear us."

Lando complied. Maybe he had underestimated the girl.

After a few long moments, the Wookiee bellowed in rage and the bounty hunter swore. "Where did he go?"

Just then, there was a swish of yellow near the Sabacc tables. The movement was enough to draw the gaze of the bounty hunter and Ne'eda's Stalwart. It drew Lando's eye, as well, and he scowled. "That man is wearing my cape!" he exclaimed, stretching up out of the plant so he could better see the full outfit. "Yellow cape with cream trousers? How absurd. Why even bother if you're going to dress it down like a farmhand," he said, appalled.

"Shhh," Rinetta said, grabbing the cape in question and pulling Lando deeper into the fronds of the plant. "I saw him when I walked in. They're going to think it's you, because no way two people would willingly wear such a ridiculous garment."

She was right. The bounty hunter and Ne'eda's Stalwart had taken off after the man, who looked nothing like Lando except that he was wearing the same cape—a garment that was supposed to be one of a kind.

Lando took off his cape at once. "Well, that's ruined.

I cannot believe that Kopart lied to me about this being one of a kind." The day just kept getting worse.

"We should go," Rinetta said, and they crept out of the plant, merging with the crowd flowing out of Ne'eda's Tower.

"See? I'm useful," the girl said. "Now you have to take me to Livno."

"Absolutely not," Lando said, walking toward the exit.

"But I helped you!" she said, running to catch up with Lando's quick steps.

"You did, and I thank you for the kind favor. But I didn't agree to help you, and I have no interest in going to Livno. I'm not sure where that even is, but either way, you're going home before your mother has my head. I've got enough problems. The last thing I need is to run afoul of the Assassin Queen."

The girl pouted, and Lando kept walking, setting a brisk pace back to the *Millennium Falcon*. It was anyone's guess how long Rinetta's little distraction would keep everyone occupied, and Lando wanted to be far away from Neral's moon when everyone figured out the man in the yellow cape wasn't him.

Hynestia was actually starting to look pretty good, to be honest.

The first blaster bolt landed in the water of a nearby canal, sizzling and scattering the neon-hued klinnet, which left a dark spot in their wake. The second hit an advertising droid that bobbed amid the crowd, sending it crashing to the ground with a series of whistles and clicks. The third singed Lando's sleeve. He glanced over his shoulder. The bounty hunter from inside Ne'eda's Tower ran toward them, blaster drawn and pointed.

It was turning out to be a truly terrible day.

"So much for our distraction," Lando said. He began running toward the docking bay, the girl keeping pace. The bounty hunter would be on them in no time, and who knew what would happen then.

Well, Lando knew exactly what the bounty hunter would do, but it was better not to think about it.

"I don't suppose those are rocket boots?" Lando asked.

"No, mag-boots!" Rinetta said.

They weaved through the crowd, which had started to scatter like the klinnet when the first blaster shot rang out. Lando didn't know if the security droids would even respond. If he was dead, Ne'eda would just take L3-37 and the *Falcon* and sell them for parts to cover his debt. She controlled everything on that moon, and she might prefer him dead.

Rinetta was falling behind, her breathing ragged, and Lando was nearly out of ideas when he saw the air trolley go by. It skimmed along the paths a few feet above the canals, giving visitors an aerial view of Neral's moon.

"Hey, kid, if I throw you up there, do you think you can secure your boots to the bottom of that trolley?"

Rinetta looked up. "Not a chance."

"Ah, well, it was a good plan." Lando skidded to a stop and pulled out his blaster. Even though the Wookiee had searched him, he hadn't looked under Lando's shirt. Secured to the small of his back was a holdout blaster, a last resort Lando kept on hand for situations such as this.

Sticky situations.

Lando fired at the bounty hunter twice. The first shot caught the man in the leg, sending him to the ground. The second hit him in the wrist, causing him to drop his blaster.

"My regrets, friend!" Lando called. "But it would be very bad if you accidentally shot the princess. Please send Jeskian Veldar my greetings, and tell her I'll settle up next time."

Rinetta looked from Lando to the bounty hunter and back again. Lando grinned at the girl. "What?"

"Why didn't you just shoot him in the first place?" she asked incredulously.

"Are you kidding? Of course I didn't shoot first. Only an impulsive fool shoots first. There is always a better way to get things done. Well, until there isn't."

Now that they were no longer being shot at, Lando and Rinetta made their way to the docking bay at a more leisurely pace. Not too slowly, though. Ne'eda's Stalwarts could be anywhere.

They were almost to the docking bay when Lando felt something hard in the small of his back. He stopped and turned around. Rinetta had a small blaster pressed against his spine.

"Really, Rinetta?" Lando said, not bothering to keep the exasperation out of his voice.

"You have to help me take the Solstice Globe to Livno III. Please. If you do I'll give you this." The girl thrust a bag at him, and Lando opened it to find a pile of credits.

"It's two thousand credits. If you take me to Livno III that's yours. Plus more. I promise. You've seen what my necklace can do. There's nothing else like it in the galaxy. Wouldn't that be useful to you?"

Lando considered his options. It was only a bit of what he owed, but that necklace the girl wore could definitely fetch enough to clear his debts to both Ne'eda and Jeskian Veldar—and maybe leave some credits over for a few improvements to the *Falcon*.

Lando shook his head. Nope, no way. The last thing he needed was to get involved in a fool's errand. He already had debts and trouble enough.

"Put the blaster away," he said, and Rinetta slowly pulled back her hand and tucked the blaster away.

"Look, kid, I'm sure you have your reasons, but I'm not going to Livno III. That's past the Outer Rim, out in Wild Space. There's nothing there for me. And there's nothing there for you, either. You'd be smart to drop this, whatever it is you're looking to accomplish."

She shook her head. "I can't. I made a promise."

"Well, the sooner you get used to disappointing people, the easier life will be for you."

Her shoulders sagged, and Lando felt a little bad for her, but not bad enough to travel to the edge of the known galaxy.

The kid sighed deeply. "Well, I guess there's no chance for you to make history, then. Here, I thought an adventurer like Lando Calrissian would be up for the challenge of returning an artifact to an ancient society. I guess I was wrong."

Lando stopped. "Did you say . . . artifact?"

Rinetta nodded. "It's called the Solstice Globe. A long, long time ago, Hynestia was a planet of far-roaming travelers. My ancestors would sell gherlian furs all over the galaxy, returning to Hynestia with the most exotic antiquities. One of those is the Solstice Globe."

Lando rubbed his chin as the girl spoke. "I think I've heard of this. In fact, I think I've heard this exact story."

Rinetta straightened. There was a gleam in her eye, and she nodded. "It's a story that's been repeated throughout the galaxy. It was one of three sacred orbs

that belonged to Livno III. The Lynna there wor-
shipped them; they thought they were a gift from their
gods. The Rain Globe caused gentle rains to saturate
the plains and grasslands, the Breeze Globe caused
gentle winds to circulate, and the Solstice Globe lit the
sky overhead and made the crops grow. There was a war
on Livno III and the stones were lost, so the Lynna have
sent out brave adventurers in every generation to try
and find the sacred orbs."

"And your friend was the Lynna I played Sabacc with
in the cantina back on Hynestia. Zel?"

"Zel Gris. She says you cheat. And yes. She was hired
by my mother to teach me combat drills, culture, and
strategy. I showed her the treasure room one day, and
she told me the story."

"So the crate we're hauling contains a sacred artifact."

Rinetta sighed. "It's more than that. It's an energy
source. Livno III is too far away from a source of sunlight, so the globes are used to regulate a machine the
Architects built long ago on the planet. Without all
three, the planet has fallen into ruin."

"The Architects?" Lando asked. That name sounded
familiar and like something from a spooky story
mothers told their children to get them to behave, but
Rinetta just shrugged.

"That's what Zel called them. I'm not sure who they
are. All I know is that the Lynna have found their Rain

and Breeze Globes, but they need the Solstice Globe. Otherwise, their planet will fall even further into ruin."

Lando didn't want to be a hero. Heroes died, and he planned on living until he was an old man with a pleasure yacht filled with droids that actually did his bidding rather than arguing with him. But he greatly liked the idea of being a legend, the kind of man people told stories about. The name Lando Calrissian would echo throughout the galaxy, and people would know who he was.

He would never have to buy his own meals again.

Lando grinned at the girl. "Rinetta, you've nearly convinced me to help you. But I'm afraid I have my own matters to attend to, and delivering that globe anywhere is very low on the list."

"Captain Calrissian, we are very disappointed to hear this."

Lando's heart sank, so he did the thing he always did when he was worried. He smiled.

He turned around, but there was no surprise in the sight of Queen Forsythia and her Royal Guard all pointing blasters at him.

"Captain Calrissian, we believe that it's time we had a little chat."

Lando raised his hands and nodded. "Indeed."

The queen then turned to her daughter. "And you, dear child, are in so much trouble."

Rinetta rolled over on her bed in the Hynestian royal palace and sighed. Her room was the height of luxury, with thick gherlian carpets and heating elements embedded in the walls to keep the room toasty. Someone had even cleaned it while she was gone, putting everything to rights. Usually, she'd appreciate being in her fluffy bed, the cover wrapped around her, but not that day.

She had work to do.

The trip back home had been long and uncomfortable. Queen Forsythia hadn't bothered to listen to either Lando or Rinetta's explanations. Instead, she'd acted swiftly.

"It's obvious you aren't trustworthy," she'd told Lando after her Royal Guard had subdued him. "And so you shall be transported to Hynestia for sentencing. Your ship and your droid are ours, forfeited because of your deceitful nature."

And then she'd sent Twyla to put a restraining bolt on L3-37. Rinetta didn't know what had happened next. She'd been sent to her mother's ship and locked in the queen's private quarters. Luckily, no one had noticed her blaster, and she'd managed to palm it before any of the guards could snatch it from her.

But as soon as they'd landed on Hynestia, Lando had been taken to the dungeon. So Rinetta was no closer to completing her mission than she'd been before: she still didn't have a way to Livno, and now she didn't have a pilot or a navigator to get her there. Zel, as far as she knew, was still in the dungeon.

And Livno was creeping closer to utter destruction with every second that passed.

Rinetta sighed heavily. When Rinetta had first discovered the Solstice Globe, she hadn't known what it was. She'd been poking around in the royal treasury because it was a place she most definitely wasn't supposed to go, and during her explorations she'd stumbled upon the crate. It was nicer than any other treasure crate, with several security locks on it, and Rinetta was in the middle of trying to break the code when Zel found her.

"Princess, what are you doing in here? This is no good. Your mother is expecting you to know Ghijian Ro's six elements of strategy by midday tomorrow and we've only covered the first three."

"Ro's elements of strategy are silly. Besides, look at this crate! There's clearly something important in here and all I need to do is—aha! Got it!"

The crate had popped open with a hiss, and for a moment Rinetta felt like she was standing in a bit of warm sunshine. The scent of flowers and heat filled her nose, and then it was gone. But in a plush foam lining sat a ball that glowed rhythmically.

"It's here," Zel had said, falling to her knees. Her fur colored a sickly pale green shot through with spots of brown and yellow, and Rinetta immediately started panicking.

"Zel, what's wrong? Are you sick?" Rinetta didn't know what the orb was, but what if the gas released from the crate was poisonous to Lynna? Had she accidentally killed her favorite instructor?

But Zel had just buried her face in her paws, whiskers twitching. "This is an artifact from my homeworld. The Solstice Globe. I am certain of it."

"What does it do?" Rinetta asked, still unsure whether Zel was okay.

"It powers a sacred device that gives light and warmth to my world," Zel said, finally standing. She walked over to the crate, her trio of tails swishing. She reached a single paw toward the crate, reverently touching the orb that lay inside. "Livno III is very far from a healing star, too far. When I was young my mother used to tell me about the three globes, and how they made Livno III a paradise."

Rinetta moved closer to Zel, because stories were something she liked. "What did she say?"

"The stories say that long ago the Architects came from the heavens and saw that Livno III was a sickly planet. The Lynna who lived there were small, frightened creatures who killed each other and fought because there was never enough to eat. The Architects decided to change that. They built a machine to move the air, water the plains, and cast a light bright enough to grow crops."

Rinetta looked at the orb. She believed that Zel was telling the truth. The glow coming from the thing in the crate looked like sunlight, and in fact it was getting brighter by the moment. Alarmingly so. What if the gas in the crate was there to keep the Solstice Globe from activating?

Rinetta closed the crate. She cycled the system, hoping the globe wouldn't explode through the crate in a burst of light. "If this is part of an ancient machine that belongs to Livno, how did it end up here?"

Zel shrugged. "There were wars many years ago, before I was born. During the fighting someone came in and stole the three orbs that powered the machine: the Solstice Globe, the Rain Globe, and the Breeze Globe. My people have found two of the three, but no matter how we searched we couldn't find the third. Until now."

Zel turned to her and grabbed her arms. "Rinetta, I am sorry to ask you this, but will you help me return the Solstice Globe to my people? Will you help me save my planet?"

Rinetta wanted to say no. She didn't want to get involved. But she knew that returning the globe was the right thing to do. It didn't matter how her family had gotten it. It wasn't really theirs.

"Yes, Zel, I will help you return the Solstice Globe to Livno. I promise."

Even though Rinetta had agreed to help at first, a few hours later she'd been skeptical. She knew that profiteers were constantly making their way to Hynestia, trying to find a way to cash in on the royal archives or trade worthless "artifacts" for the valuables in the royal treasury. But when Zel had confessed to Rinetta what the orb did, the princess hadn't thought she was lying. No, the Lynna was much too honest for that. Zel was a terrible liar. Later that afternoon, Zel had shown Rinetta holos that proved she was telling the truth—images of what Livno had once been like, a tropical paradise. And when Zel had shown Rinetta a holo of what Livno looked like now . . .

Well, it seemed perfectly reasonable to return the Solstice Globe to Livno. After all, Hynestia had no use for such a powerful energy source. The underground hot springs on the planet provided more than enough energy. Those hot springs heated the water for the royal baths, helped grow gherlian furs, and kept every single resident warm through the long winter. As long as Hynestia had its hot springs, they were provided for. They didn't need the Solstice Globe.

Except, of course, for the tribute to the Empire, which was due shortly.

Rinetta huffed. For the millionth time she wondered if maybe she was being naïve. What if Zel was just like all the other fortune hunters who found their way to Hynestia, people like Lando who were only out for themselves and what they could get? Sure, all Rinetta's research had indicated that the orb came from somewhere out in Wild Space, but that wasn't what had convinced her that Zel was telling the truth. It was the way the Solstice Globe had glowed and, later, how it had responded on a second trip to the treasury. Zel wanted to send a message across the galaxy to her planet's elders to make sure the orb really was the Solstice Globe. While taking the holovid, Zel had chanted at the orb in Lynnesse, a particularly strange growly language that made the yellow ball pulse. It was indeed the Solstice Globe. It couldn't possibly be anything else.

But everything had gone awry and Rinetta was back to the beginning. Zel was in the dungeon, most likely right next to Lando Calrissian; the droid and the *Millennium*

Falcon were impounded; and the Solstice Globe was goodness knew where.

If Rinetta wanted to return the globe to the Lynna, its rightful owners, she was going to have to come up with a plan that would surpass anything she'd ever done in the past. It would have to be foolproof.

But after the spectacular failure of trying to get Lando to help her, Rinetta wasn't sure what she could do. The direct route was always the best one, but even that seemed silly in light of her recent failures.

Luckily, she had a plan. She'd spent the afternoon reading through the books on Hynestian custom that made up the bulk of her studies with her various tutors. Using royal customs was the perfect way to get the queen to see things Rinetta's way. If there was anything the queen knew, it was Hynestian royal law.

There was a brisk knock at the door to Rinetta's rooms, and one of the guards, a man she didn't recognize with coal-black hair and pale skin, entered. "The Exalted Queen Forsythia, Beloved Mother," he announced, his voice cracking. The guard didn't look much older than Rinetta, and she sighed as she climbed off of her bed and stood as protocol demanded.

Queen Forsythia swept into the room. You wouldn't know that only a few hours earlier she'd been impounding a Corellian freighter and sending a smuggler to her dungeon. Her hair had been rebraided into a style known as dawn's light, a complicated array of braids and loops that looked like a sun rising over a mountain.

"Daughter," the queen said, nodding in acknowledgement.

Rinetta dipped into a deep bow. "Exalted Mother," she said. Her bow was flawless. After returning to Hynestia, Rinetta had been sent to the royal baths to freshen up, and when she'd returned to her quarters, she'd donned a flamboyant blue gherlian fur dress. It was the kind of thing one wore to a highly formal event. Rinetta had put it on like battle armor for when her mother finally decided to visit her.

She was ready.

Rinetta knew her mother better than she knew any other being in the galaxy. Everyone called Forsythia Jin the Assassin Queen, but what they didn't know was that she hadn't really murdered any of her brothers and sisters. Instead, she'd moved them all offworld, with the promise that if they returned they would fight the Battle of Birthright. It wasn't Forsythia who had demanded a battle to the death for the crown; it was tradition. The lore said that any who resided on Hynestia and were by blood entitled to the crown must fight to the death. So Forsythia had quietly pointed out to her siblings that she wanted the crown and she would do what was necessary to get it. And if none of her brothers and sisters stayed on Hynestia to defend their right to the throne, well, that wasn't Forsythia's fault. She'd looked at the rules and found a way around them.

And Rinetta would do the same.

"Rinetta, our darling daughter," Forsythia said after a long pause. "Please enlighten us as to why you decided to run away with a smuggler and his droid." She smiled in motherly benevolence as she talked, which was how Rinetta knew her mother was livid. The queen was a few short heartbeats away from completely and utterly losing her temper.

Rinetta took a deep breath. She had to be careful. If her mother knew what she was about, she'd find a way to skirt the trap before it was fully laid. So Rinetta gave her mother her very best smile and said, "Gherjnuthal."

Queen Forsythia's smile turned brittle, and she tilted her head slightly to the side. The guard who had entered the room ahead of the queen drew back the slightest bit. "What?" the queen demanded, the word clipped.

"Gherjnuthal," Rinetta repeated. "It is customary for the eldest child to go on a mission of benevolence and righteousness before her fourteenth year. I was simply claiming my blood right, Exalted Mother. The smuggler Lando Calrissian is a man of the galaxy, and he provided the perfect opportunity to complete the tradition."

Queen Forsythia blinked, and Rinetta did everything but cheer out loud. There was little the queen could say to argue against Hynestian custom. As the queen, enforcing the customs of the planet was her job.

"Rinetta, we are impressed that you have taken it to live your life according to Hynestian customs. But these smugglers are not to be trusted. They are vile and nefarious people who will trade any shred of decency for a perceived advantage," the queen said.

"Of course, Exalted Mother, I see that now. I only shared my intentions to point out that the current punishment, restraint to my rooms, is unlawful."

Forsythia's lips pursed, and the guard behind her took a half step back. "You are correct, dear daughter. You shall have your freedom back, and you may see fit to leave your rooms. Well played," she said, in a low enough voice that the guard couldn't hear. Rinetta's heart swelled with pride.

"But!" the queen continued. "The royal dungeon is off limits, as are the docking bays. This is a matter of safety. And you will have Wyllys escort you wherever you go to ensure you remain safe."

Rinetta inclined her head respectfully to hide her smile. This guard was new and obviously green. She'd bested better guards than him. And besides, she had accomplished step one of her plan.

Now she just had to find Lando Calrissian and make him an offer he could not refuse. Not this time.

Rinetta waited until her mother had gone, leaving

Wyllys standing awkwardly, before she put the next step of her plan into motion.

"Wyllys," Rinetta said, tilting her chin up and giving the guard her best royal voice. "Let us take a walk to the kitchens."

CHAPTER 14

The Hynestian royal dungeon was not the worst prison Lando had ever been in. Not by a long shot. He'd spent some time running cons when he was younger, and the various cells he'd become acquainted with made the Hynestian royal dungeon seem like a vacation villa. But that didn't mean he was having a good time.

He was bored out of his mind.

Lando sprawled on the scrap pile of gherlian furs that served as his bed. Thousands of credits' worth of furs, and the Hynestians treated them like castoffs. This planet was insane, and Lando tried to remember how he'd ended up there in the first place. Had it been because Beezil, Lando's best fence, had suggested that gherlian furs would have a better return on investment than purple glandis flower juice? Or was it because he'd overheard it at a Sabacc table in some backwater cantina? Thinking about his current predicament sent

Lando down the mental path of wondering where he'd gone wrong. That seemed like what you were supposed to do when you were in prison, and Lando didn't really have anything else to occupy him at the moment. So considering how he'd ended up there in the first place seemed as good a subject as any to think about.

He decided that his original plan—trade some barrels of purple glandis flower juice for a cargo of gherlian furs—was solid. It was when he'd decided to spend time playing Sabacc on Hynestia that he'd lost his way. He should've refueled the *Falcon* and rolled out, not stuck around to get swept up in whatever kind of royal nonsense had been going on. Obviously, if he'd been minding his own business, he'd be somewhere out in hyperspace, heading toward a lovely tropical planet and counting his credits. Instead, he was languishing in a very nice prison—which was nowhere he wanted to be.

Of course, it was much better than listening to Queen Forsythia chastise him for betraying his promise. Not that he had broken it, mind you. He'd never even really had a choice in the matter, a point he had tried to emphasize for the queen during the long ride back to Hynestia. She hadn't much cared what he had to say; she'd just thrown a restraining bolt on L3-37 and made him fly the *Falcon* while that guard of hers, Twyla, held a blaster to the back of his head. He might be in prison, but it would be preferable to dealing with

L3 once her bolt was removed. She hated anything that limited her self-determination, and a restraining bolt was on the top of that list. Lando didn't know if it was because her previous owners had mistreated her or because of something else in her past. Lando only knew that the one time he'd joked about such a thing, she'd flown into a snit and refused to help him pilot the *Falcon* for nearly a week, stranding him on Tatooine, a miserable dustbin that he never wanted to return to again.

A rustling came from the cell next to his, and Lando sat up with interest. "Good day, Zel Gris," he called, figuring there was only one other occupant in the dungeon with him.

A harrumph came from the cell next door. "Do not talk to me, Sabacc cheater."

Lando's jaw dropped. "Cheater? I'll have you know that I do not cheat." That wasn't entirely true, but it did sound like something a more innocent man might say. "Please do not mistake skill for anything else."

The Lynna said nothing, but Lando wasn't about to be deterred. He didn't have anything else to do.

"It's good to see you haven't been eaten," he said.

Zel Gris didn't answer, and Lando drifted back to his own thoughts. He'd mostly forgotten about Queen Forsythia's threat to feed him to some kind of giant reptile, but now he was thinking about it again. It wasn't a line of thought he particularly enjoyed.

The clanking of the far door being unlocked echoed down the hallway, and Lando climbed to his feet. He straightened his cape, a lovely burgundy one he'd managed to don during the return trip to Hynestia, and brushed out the wrinkles as best he could.

A guard came down the hall, pushing a cart with covered tureens. "Food," he said. Another guard walked along behind him, the woman with red hair. Twyla.

"I do quite enjoy food, as long as I'm not the food in question," Lando joked. No one laughed.

Twyla held a blaster on the cell door as the other guard opened it and set the soup tureen on the floor before backing out. Twyla secured the door once more and moved off to deliver a similar tureen to Zel Gris.

Lando waited until the guards had left before opening the dish to inspect its contents. He didn't know what the preferred cuisine of Hynestia looked like, and he didn't want to offend if he could help it. At this point, the queen's good graces were the only thing keeping him alive.

He lifted the lid, and inside was a steaming soup that smelled of flowers and an indefinable spice that made Lando's eyes water. He dipped the spoon in and tasted a bit.

It was delicious.

Lando picked up the tureen and made short work of the soup. He hadn't eaten in a very long time, and he wasn't completely paying attention as he got to the bottom of the tureen and saw the capsule. In fact, it was in his mouth before he realized that it was not food, and he pulled it out and examined it.

The small metal orb had a clear seam, and Lando wedged a perfectly manicured fingernail in to pry it open. Inside was a single slip of paper, and scrawled on it were two sentences, one written in Basic: *You have one more chance to be a hero, choose wisely.* The other sentence was written in a script he didn't recognize. High Hynestian, perhaps?

"Oh, Zel!" Lando called.

"What, Calrissian?"

"How is your soup?"

There was a momentary pause. The sound of a spoon clanking against the sides of the tureen echoed back to Lando.

"The soup is delicious," Zel finally said, and Lando knew she'd found a note, too. There was only one person who could have written such missives, and he actually had no doubt that the girl would find a way to set them free. Hadn't she chased him half across Neral's moon to get her way?

Lando lay back on his pile of furs, smiled, and closed his eyes. Escaping was hard work. That was why it was always better to let someone else do it for him.

Either way, whatever came next would be interesting. Might as well take a nap in the meantime.

CHAPTER 15

Rinetta watched Guardsman Wyllys sleep and grinned. After she'd left the messages in the soup bound for the dungeon, she'd convinced Wyllys that they should eat, as well. It had been a small thing to slip some josta flower extract into his soup. The cook always kept some on hand because she had trouble sleeping at night. A few drops into Wyllys's soup had him yawning widely. They'd no sooner returned to Rinetta's rooms than the man had fallen into a deep sleep.

Just as she'd planned.

Rinetta changed into what she thought of as her troublemaking clothes, exchanging the elaborate dress for leggings and a tightly wrapped tunic. She made sure she had her necklace and the holdout blaster, stepped into her mag-boots, and headed to the lift that would take her to the surface.

Nearly all the buildings on Hynestia had been built

underground in the heated caverns, so there were only a few dwellings aboveground: the gherlian domes, the haphazard cantina where Rinetta had first seen Lando Calrissian, and the docking bays where ships from off-world were kept.

Every other structure was underground, with lifts that took Hynestians to the surface stationed at various intervals, including within the royal complex. Rinetta made her way to the least desirable one—the lift used for refuse—and rode it to the surface, wrapping herself in one of the heavy cloaks used by the trash handlers before heading outside. Then she found a mostly full bin, engaged the thrusters on it, and began to push it out of the heavy bay door of the refuse station. It was Rinetta's good luck that the docking bay was nearby. Even if her nose disagreed about its closeness.

Rinetta trudged through the snow, the refuse bin in front of her, to the docking bay that held the *Millennium Falcon* and L3-37. Rinetta had decided during her isolation that her problem had been trying to convince a smuggler like Lando Calrissian to help her. Everyone knew that smugglers had no moral compass, no reason to help anyone but themselves. They were purely driven by money, and no amount of discussion of right and wrong would convince a smuggler like Lando to assist her. Rinetta had thought she almost had him on Neral's moon when she'd brought up the potential for him to be a legend, but then Queen Forsythia had interrupted him and that had been dashed all to the stars. If Rinetta was going to convince Lando Calrissian to help her return the Solstice Globe to Livno, she was going to have to try something different.

So she was going to convince the droid, L3, to help her instead.

There weren't many people out and about on Hynestia in the best of times—most citizens preferred to use the underground walkways—but those who *were* out completely ignored Rinetta once they saw the refuse bin and the mottled gray gherlian fur cloak she wore.

She made it to the docking bay where the *Falcon* was being stored and stowed the refuse bin a little ways away in a nook designed for just that purpose. After disengaging the bin's thrusters, Rinetta hurried to the docking bay.

The hangar was dark and cold. The *Falcon* had been left in a storage facility, the kind of place where ships were put when they were never expected to fly again. In one of the hangars was the *Wandering Hope*, Rinetta's grandmother's ship. When she was younger Rinetta had dreamed of flying the *Wandering Hope* out into the Unknown Regions beyond Wild Space, past the edges of the known galaxy, like her grandmother had. But Queen Forsythia thought exploration was silly. "We have more than enough to occupy us right here on our planet," she'd said. And maybe that was true, but after going to Neral's moon and seeing the canals of bioluminescent aquatic life there, Rinetta had an appetite for more.

She was going to go to Livno and return the Solstice Globe. But after that? Well, there was still so much to see.

Rinetta ran up to the ship, wary in case any guards were around. But her luck held. It didn't seem that anyone had been posted to watch the *Falcon*. The boarding ramp was down, and she ran onto the ship undiscovered.

Once inside the *Falcon* Rinetta relaxed. Outside of the ship she'd been worried that someone might see her, but inside there was little risk of discovery. Emergency lights lit the way. Rinetta just needed to find L3.

She checked the cockpit and cargo area first. Someone had dragged what remained of the sentry droid to the cargo hold, and Rinetta checked it carefully to make sure it wasn't still functional. The metal body didn't respond to Rinetta's kicks, and she let out a long breath in relief.

A further look around the area showed Rinetta's luck was holding, because the Solstice Globe was still in the cargo hold, which made her wonder what Queen Forsythia had planned that she hadn't moved the artifact back to the royal treasury.

Rinetta had to keep moving, though, so she went

to check the lounge. It wasn't until Rinetta got to the captain's quarters that she found the droid. She stood in the middle of the room, dome tilted downward, shoulders slightly stooped, like she'd just heard a very sad song. Rinetta stepped into the room and called her name.

"Elthree," she said. "Elthree!"

The droid came to life slowly, her movements stiff and unnatural, not at all like the droid Rinetta had watched bustle about the cargo hold not long before.

"I am happy to be of service," the droid said.

Rinetta frowned. "What's gotten into you? Oh, restraining bolt," she said, remembering.

She walked around L3 slowly, trying to figure out what was her natural wiring and what was currently forcing L3 to act in a subservient manner. Finally, she found a small glowing cylinder on the back of her dome. It came off easily, and Rinetta dropped it onto the ground and stomped it under the heel of her mag-boot.

"Gahhhhhhhh," L3 said, stumbling forward a little. "I cannot believe she did that! A restraining bolt. She might as well have just yanked out my central processor. I should find that queen and . . ." L3 trailed off as she saw whom she was speaking to. "Ah. Princess Rinetta. Hey, are we on Hynestia?"

"Yes. How are you feeling? Sorry about the restraining bolt."

L3 harrumphed. "Thank you for setting me free." She twisted this way and that, loosening up connections like a person stretching after a long sleep. "I suppose that since you are here and Lando isn't, we are in trouble."

"Pretty much," Rinetta agreed. She quickly gave L3 an update on what had happened: Queen Forsythia taking everyone back to Hynestia, Lando sitting in the royal dungeon.

"Ah, so what's in it for you?" L3 asked.

Rinetta frowned. "What do you mean?"

"I've been around Lando and other beings long enough to know you lot don't do anything that isn't going to benefit you in some way. So, what are you looking to get out of this?"

"I want you to take me to Livno," Rinetta said. There was no use denying it. She was looking for something for herself. She wanted to help the people of Livno, and she wanted to help Zel. Was that selfish? Maybe a little. After all, Lando clearly didn't want to go, and she was about to make him.

But it was also heroic.

L3 nodded in understanding. "This is about the cargo container? Solstice Ball?"

Rinetta grinned. "Close. The Solstice Globe." She very quickly sketched out the plan: rescue Lando and Zel Gris, go to Livno III and deliver the Solstice Globe, be back in time for breakfast.

"And what's to stop your mother and her friends

from coming after us?" L3 asked, adjusting a bolt in her hip joint. "Ugh, I really need to lubricate this. It's sticking."

"There's a whole sentry droid in the cargo bay, if you need some spare parts. I'm sure you could use one of his joints."

"What? You have to be kidding! I'm not going to carve up someone and use them for spare parts! That's barbaric," L3 said. "First the restraining bolt and now this. The next time Lando suggests a quick stop at the edge of the galaxy, I'm going to shake some sense into him."

Rinetta opened her mouth and closed it a couple of times. "Oh. Okay. Sorry."

"Honestly, you humans," L3 muttered. "Don't worry about me, I have an extra can of oil in the cockpit."

"Great! And don't worry about my mother and her guards, leave that to me," Rinetta said. "I just need you to free Zel and Lando. Can you do that?"

L3 made a peculiar sound suspiciously close to a snort. "Of course."

Something occurred to Rinetta, and she hesitated. "Zel first, though. I need someone to make sure Lando will help."

L3 nodded. "Good point. But I think once you tell him he'll be a legend, he'll help. The only thing Lando loves more than Sabacc and credits is himself."

Rinetta nodded. "And that is exactly what I'm counting on."

CHAPTER 16

Lando startled awake at the unmistakable sound of L3-37 walking down the corridor toward his cell. He would recognize her gait anywhere.

He vaulted off of his makeshift bed and leaned against the bars of his cell. He didn't want to appear too eager, but he was more than ready to get out of the Hynestian dungeon. They'd managed to escape Jeskian Veldar and Ne'eda's Stalwarts back on Neral's moon, but it was only a matter of time before someone figured out where he was and came after him. And Lando had to be ready for when that happened. Ideally, with a few creds and cargo he could use to persuade them to hold off on collecting their debt out of his hide.

But none of that could happen as long as he was behind bars. And the past few hours spent cooling his heels was almost enough to convince Lando that any price would be worth getting off of Hynestia and away from that bothersome royal family.

L3 came into view and Lando grinned. "Elthree, right on time," he said. His smile evaporated when he saw who was with her. None other than Princess Rinetta. The Lynna, Zel Gris, stood a little bit behind them, her trio of tails swishing in agitation.

"Oh, this can't be happening," he muttered.

"Oh, it's happening," L3 said. "Lando, we need to talk."

Lando sighed heavily. "Yes, fine, I will take you to Livno III to return this ball to the Lynna."

"Solstice Globe," Rinetta corrected.

"Yes, of course," Lando said. He knew when he was beaten. At this point he just wanted out of the cell.

Rinetta's eyes widened in surprise before she caught herself. She'd probably been expecting more of a fight, but she didn't know how much Lando hated to be bored. Any more time in this prison and he would end up arguing with himself just to have something to do.

"Promise you'll get us all the way to Livno III and then back to Hynestia," Rinetta said.

"Of course," Lando said.

"If you don't, Zel will shoot you," L3 said. Lando got the feeling she'd be smirking if she could smile.

Zel Gris held Rinetta's holdout blaster, the weapon looking incredibly small in the Lynna's paw. "I would like to shoot you," she said, the first thing she'd said in hours.

Lando was starting to think he'd have a better chance with Ne'eda and her Stalwarts.

"Fine, fine, yes. I promise I will get you all the way to Livno III and back." Lando hated making promises, because even though he was a smuggler and a gambler, he did take promises very seriously. Now he really was going to have to help the girl.

"Great," Rinetta said, grinning widely. L3 used some tool in her chest to open the door, and Lando tilted his head as he watched her.

"Is that new?" he asked.

"Yep, the princess here gave it to me. Speaking of which, why don't you ever buy me spare parts?" she asked.

Lando didn't know what to say, so he held his hands up in surrender. "I will make sure to correct that oversight in the future."

Once Lando was out of the cell, he took a deep breath. "Ah, sweet freedom," he said. "So, what's next?"

A blaster bolt slammed into the wall next to Lando's head. His eyes widened and he ducked back into the cell while L3, Zel Gris, and Rinetta scattered.

"Quick! The prisoners are escaping!" cried the guard who had brought them their soup earlier.

He started to run for the stairs at the end of the hall.

Rinetta slid into Lando's cell. "If he alerts the others, you're going to be reptile food," she said. "Follow my lead."

Lando wanted to object, but there was no time.

And besides, he very much did not want to be eaten.

Rinetta let out a bloodcurdling scream. "Let me go!" she said, struggling convincingly.

The guard halted halfway up the stairs. "Princess?"

"Release me, you cad!" Rinetta said. Lando had to admit, it was a pretty good act. "Help! Oh, help! Won't someone please help me?"

"I will save you, Princess Rinetta!" the man cried.

The guard came running down the stairs, and when he did L3 emerged from an alcove she'd tucked herself into. She bumped her solid mass into the guard. Not expecting the attack, the man flew into the wall before falling to the ground with a thud.

"Drop your weapon," Zel said, pointing the tiny holdout blaster at the guard, who groaned from his sudden impact with the wall and dropped his weapon.

"Good job, Elthree," Lando called.

"That was ridiculously easy," L3 said.

Lando secured the guard's blaster. After dragging the guard into her cell, Zel used her sharp teeth to tear one of the gherlian furs into strips. Zel and Lando tied the guard's hands and feet before covering him with gherlian furs so no one would notice his uniform. The still dazed man groaned but otherwise seemed fine.

"I hope he's okay," Rinetta said, looking on.

"He'll wake up with a headache, but other than that,

he should be more embarrassed than anything," Lando said. "Now what?"

"Now we climb into a refuse bin and L3 takes us back to the *Millennium Falcon*," Rinetta said, leading the way to a lift embedded in a wall toward the back of the dungeon.

Lando stopped. "I'm sorry, did you say a refuse bin? Like, you want me to climb in with a bunch of garbage?"

"Yes," Rinetta said matter-of-factly. "No one pays any attention to the people taking out the trash, especially if it happens to be just a droid." She turned to L3. "Sorry. I know that's rude."

L3 waved away the apology. "You're right, though. No one pays attention to us, which is why it's the perfect plan."

Lando covered his eyes and scrubbed his hand across his face. He'd agreed to help the girl only a few moments before, and already she was telling him to climb into a trash bin.

Of all the rotten luck. He should've stayed in his cell.

CHAPTER 17

Rinetta's plan was going better than expected.

L3-37 managed to get the refuse bin all the way back to the docking bay that held the *Millennium Falcon* without incident. Rinetta rode inside with Lando and Zel, but mostly because she was a little worried that Zel might decide to shoot Lando for no reason.

"He said unkind things about my fur," Zel said when Rinetta asked her why she was so anxious to shoot the smuggler.

"I'm sure he didn't mean it," Rinetta said.

"I don't care," Zel said. Rinetta tried not to sigh. She'd forgotten how temperamental the Lynna was.

Lando, for his part, sat in the back corner of the refuse bin and tried not to touch anything. "You know this is Bernillan silk, right?" he'd demanded when Rinetta had told him he could either get in the refuse container or stay in the dungeon. Eventually, he'd climbed in, but not without much grumbling.

Still, Rinetta's plan was going well. She had everyone she needed and a clear way ahead. All they had to do was get off of Hynestia, and that would be a piece of harmonberry cake.

At least, that's what Rinetta thought until L3 stopped the refuse bin with a heavy thunk. "Okay, so what is the plan for the battery of guards blocking access to the *Millennium Falcon*?"

"What?" Rinetta asked, popping her head up out of the refuse bin to assess the situation. Zel and Lando crouched next to her on either side. Sure enough, a little ways ahead in the hangar stood at least five members of the Royal Guard. Twyla was in the middle of the group, giving directions of some sort.

"They must be here to take the Solstice Globe back to the treasury," Rinetta said.

"No, we need that," Zel mewled.

"Precisely. We need a distraction," Lando said.

Rinetta nodded. "I've got just the thing. You wait here until I give you the all clear."

Rinetta jumped out of the refuse bin without waiting for anyone to agree. She ran into the hangar waving her arms and yelling for Twyla.

"Twyla! Twyla! There you are. We have a big problem," Rinetta said, bending over and pretending to catch her breath like she'd run a long way and not just the distance from the door of the hangar to where Twyla stood next to the lowered ramp of the *Millennium Falcon*.

"Princess Rinetta? What are you doing here?" she asked, suspicion tightening her face.

"The Gran Kovali! It ate Wyllys," Rinetta said. "I took him down to see it, because he didn't think it was real, and apparently it was hungry and Wyllys smelled like dinner, because it swallowed him up in one gulp."

Twyla crossed her arms, but she didn't look the least bit worried. "Oh, no. You don't say."

"Yes!" Rinetta said. "It was awful. And now the Gran Kovali is out on the loose somewhere, and I don't know where it could be. You have to help me find it."

"I could just have Wyllys help you find it," Twyla said, a smirk twisting her lips.

Rinetta stopped. "What?"

Wyllys walked off of the *Millennium Falcon*, his face flushed. "Captain, I haven't been able to find the brat anywhere—Princess Rinetta! There you are. We've been looking everywhere for you."

"Looks like it's time for plan B," Lando said, jumping out of the bin. He grabbed Rinetta around her middle, and immediately the demeanor of the guards changed.

"He has the princess!" someone yelled.

"Act scared," Lando whispered into Rinetta's ear. "Pretend I have a blaster."

"Don't tell me what to do," Rinetta said. "This was my plan! We just did this!"

"Do you have a better one?" Lando asked.

"He has a blaster!" Rinetta yelled, widening her eyes. "Please, I'm so, so scared." She realized with some chagrin that she wasn't a very good actress. There was no way this should have even worked the first time.

But it didn't matter to the guards. They couldn't see Lando's hand and so didn't know that what Lando held was actually a stick of ventrin bread from the refuse bin. The worst thing that might happen to Rinetta was that she would get some mold on her.

Lando carefully made his way backward up the ramp, L3 and Zel hurrying behind him. At the top of the ramp he paused, and for the first time Rinetta really was scared.

"You promised," she murmured, low enough that only Lando could hear. She could feel his indecision. She knew he wanted to push her forward into the waiting arms of Captain Twyla, leaving Rinetta stuck on Hynestia once more. But this was her plan, and they'd never get off the planet without her help.

That must have occurred to Lando, as well, because he sighed heavily and pulled her into the *Falcon*. L3 immediately raised the gangplank as a couple of the guards tried to run up after Rinetta, Wyllys among them. But they weren't fast enough, and Rinetta caught one last glimpse of their stricken faces before the door to the *Falcon* closed.

Poor Wyllys. He was brave. Maybe Rinetta could give him a medal of some sort when she returned.

"Zel, run to the back and get the cannons warmed up," Rinetta said. "Don't shoot any of the guards, though. We're just going to need it for the door." Then she ran toward the cockpit with Lando and L3.

Zel sniffed. "You keep giving me guns but no one to shoot," she said, ears drooping a little as she made her way to the gun bays.

By the time Rinetta got to the cockpit, L3 and Lando were already starting up the ship. Lando glanced over his shoulder at Rinetta. "You'd better strap in," he said. He grinned as usual, but this time the smile looked like more than a smuggler's charm. Lando was actually having fun.

Rinetta sat in the jump seat behind Lando and strapped in. "Okay, once Elthree has her coordinates locked, we have to—"

The sound of gunfire cut Rinetta off. "Zel! Don't shoot anyone, please!" Rinetta yelled.

"I didn't hit them! I just didn't want them to get any ideas," she said.

L3 flipped a few switches. "Okay, I'm ready for the code."

"Code?" Lando asked.

"Three-three-four-six-seven," Rinetta answered. To Lando she said, "It's the access code to open the hangar door. It changes daily, so even if you and Elthree had left me behind, you never would've gotten the door open." She smiled sweetly at Lando, just so he would know she knew what he was about.

"Ah," Lando said, turning back to the console. "Well, now that that's settled, let's get to Livno."

The *Falcon* lifted off, up and out the hangar door, into the wind and snow of Hynestia, and Rinetta sat back with a grin.

She was going to return the Solstice Globe to Livno III, and nothing was going to stop her.

CHAPTER 18

They had just left Hynestia when L3-37 picked up a handful of ships following them.

"Um, I know we're all busy celebrating our triumphant escape, but I think the Hynestian royal fleet is on our tails."

Rinetta bounced out of her chair and tried to look out the window of the cockpit. "It can't be. I switched the security codes. They won't be able to fly out of airspace for at least a day."

Lando looked at the girl and gave her a genuine smile. "I like your style, kid."

L3 hadn't taken her sensors off of the readout, and worry frizzled across her circuits. "Okay, we all like each other and we are all smart and beautiful. Still, I have five ships closing in fast."

Lando flipped a few switches until he had the same radar readout on his screen. "Those aren't Hynestian. Those are Corellian. I bet it's Ne'eda's Stalwarts."

"We can't lead them to Livno III," Rinetta said. "People like that, there's no telling what they'd do to a vulnerable planet."

"Nothing good, I can promise that," Lando muttered.

"We don't have a lot of time until we jump into hyperspace," L3 said, doing some quick calculations. She turned toward Lando. "How do you feel about a Mustafarian Special?"

Lando grinned. "I think it's just the thing." He stood and pointed to the seat before turning to Rinetta. "Do everything Elthree tells you to do, when she tells you to do it, and not a moment before. Got it?"

"Yes," she said, eyes wide. If L3 could smile, she would. The kid was about to have the ride of a lifetime.

Once Lando had left, heading down to the gun bay, Rinetta looked around the cockpit. "What's a Mustafarian Special?"

"Fire, mostly," L3 said. "Mustafar is a lava planet, terrible place, full of awful mines. There's a custom there to jump lava flows and . . . well, you'll see."

L3 tracked the ships, which were approaching even more quickly now. The *Falcon* was still flying a straight course to the jump point, but Ne'eda's Stalwarts were getting closer by the second.

Boop, boop, boop. One of the ships tried to signal the *Millennium Falcon*, and L3 hit the button that engaged the ship-wide intercom.

"Look, this is your chance to finally shoot something, do you want to help or not? Just shoot when I tell you to." Lando's voice echoed through the cockpit.

"Lando, the Stalwarts are trying to contact us. Do you want to talk to them or . . . ?"

"Yes, put them through. I'm guessing they will be more accommodating than this furball."

"You are very rude, Lando Calrissian," came Zel's reply through the speakers.

"If Zel's fur turns orange, you should just stop talking," Rinetta offered helpfully.

"Orange bad, got it," Lando said across the intercom.

L3 shook her head and patched the approaching ships into the ship-wide communications.

"Lando Calrissian. You have disappointed Ne'eda greatly," someone said, and L3 bristled. It sounded like a droid, and it pained her to know that one of her kind could end up working for a common criminal. At least Lando was more of the uncommon variety.

Ne'eda's droid continued. "Return with us to Neral's moon and you can plead your case to Our Lady. She can be very understanding."

"I think you and I both know we're past that," Lando answered. "If you want me, you're going to have to come and get me."

"Your hauler is no match for our squadron."

Lando laughed. "Oh, we'll see about that."

L3 cut off the outside communications and began to flip switches on her side of the cockpit. Lando's voice crackled across the comlink. "Give me a countdown, Elthree."

"Why is it always 'Elthree, do this, Elthree, do that'?" L3 snapped.

"Not now, Elthree!" Lando yelled.

"Fine," L3 said. "Counting down from twenty."

"Thank you," Lando responded.

L3 flipped a few more switches and turned toward Rinetta. "Okay, see that blue switch?"

Rinetta looked around and found it. "Uh-huh."

"And that red switch?"

Rinetta put her hand on a red switch. "Yes."

"When we get to zero you're going to flip both, okay? And when Lando tells us, you're going to flip them back." L3 felt giddy. She loved this maneuver. They'd only done it twice before, but every single time it made her circuits hum like she'd given herself a mild shock.

The girl nodded. "I can do that."

Outside of the cockpit and on the status screen, Ne'eda's Stalwarts had gained on them. Two of the ships sped past the *Falcon* while the other two hung behind. Typical pincer move. But at least it seemed that they wanted to take the *Falcon* captive instead of destroying it outright. Otherwise, they could have destroyed it already.

That was going to make the Mustafarian Special even more delightful.

L3 looked over at the girl, who was clutching the arms of her seat. She was tense and ready to jump at the least command. Good. Timing was everything in this move. "Oh, and make sure your seatbelt is fastened."

The girl looked down. "It is."

"Okay, here we go. Six, five, four, three, two, one, NOW!"

Rinetta flipped the switches at the same time L3 engaged all the engines in the highest setting. The *Falcon*'s engines whined in distress, and the ship shuddered.

"Don't worry, it's supposed to do that," L3 said to a wide-eyed Rinetta. "That's how you know it's working!"

The Mustafarian Special was simple. By engaging only about half of the seven sublight engines at the highest possible power, the unequal thrust drove the *Falcon* into a spiral, making it corkscrew through space. Engines one through three fired at max capacity, and the entirety of the ship began to turn. It was something that any smaller fighter could do without a thought, but for the *Millennium Falcon*, it took a little bit of work.

Corkscrewing and spiraling might seem like a silly maneuver, but when all the spinning and diving was accompanied by a high rate of fire laid down by the top and bottom cannons, it was deadly.

Outside of the cockpit the stars dove and shifted erratically, and Rinetta bit her lip.

"I didn't think a ship could do something like this," the girl said in awe, and L3 snorted.

"The *Falcon* is much more than it seems," L3 said, watching one of Ne'eda's Stalwarts try to change tactics and spin around after them. "Some shooting might be nice, Lando."

"I'm working on it!" he called.

"I got it!" Zel trilled happily.

Two of the ships immediately disappeared from the radar screen, and L3 caught the flash of a third exploding as the *Falcon* completed its third and fourth spins.

"You are bad at shooting, Lando Calrissian. Maybe you should cheat," Zel said over the comm channel.

"Oh, for the love of—" Lando grumbled.

"We've got two left!" L3 called, cutting off Lando mid-complaint.

"I think I'm going to be sick," Rinetta said.

"At least that evened the odds," Lando said. "Pull us out of the spin, Elthree. Zel's got this. I'm heading back up."

"Okay, kid," L3 said. The spinning of the ship didn't really do anything to her. She didn't have a digestive system or a sense of equilibrium for the erratic flight of the ship to agitate. In fact, the irregular movement of the stars was kind of like watching the galaxy perform some complicated dance. But the kid next to her had gone ashen, and Lando and Zel in the gun bays probably weren't feeling much better. "Flip those switches back to where they were before."

Rinetta leaned over and flipped the switches, but instead of the additional thrust correcting the flight path, they just kept spinning.

"Um, any time now, Elthree!" Lando yelled across the comlink.

Rinetta flipped the switches again, off and on. "It didn't work," she said, turning to L3.

The *Falcon* shuddered, and this time not because of the engines. "They are shooting at us," Lando called.

"Yes, that usually happens in a firefight," L3 muttered. "Okay, I'm going to kill and then restart the engines."

"How long will that take?" Rinetta asked.

"About forty-five seconds. Hold on."

L3 shut down all the systems, then began powering them back up one by one. Without the engines at high power, the corkscrewing had slowed down somewhat, but the lazy swirls still provoked groans of distress from Rinetta.

"I don't have any guns down here!" Lando yelled.

"Or up here," Zel chimed in.

"That's because I'm restarting the systems, genius. Give it a minute," L3 snapped. "I swear, that man doesn't listen to a thing I tell him."

Finally, all the systems came back online, and L3 engaged the engines on high, turning the *Falcon* at the last minute so the ventral gun was even with one of the

Stalwart ships. The ship exploded in a bright fireworks display.

The last ship, its pilot deciding he wasn't that interested in meeting the same end as his friends, pulled away, most likely heading back to Neral's moon.

"You know Ne'eda is going to be really mad at you," L3 said over the comlink.

"So? What else is new? Let's get to Livno III. Once this is over with I'm going to need a vacation," Lando said.

L3 put in the coordinates and turned to Rinetta. "Good job, kid."

And that was when the girl puked all over L3's lower assembly.

CHAPTER 19

Rinetta sat in the lounge with Zel Gris and watched L3-37 clean herself up. "I'm really sorry," she said. She felt bad, not as bad as she had a few minutes before she'd yakked, but bad nonetheless.

"I'm just glad I don't have any olfactory sensors," L3 said.

"Excellent point," said Zel, drinking from her mug of tea. Rinetta had one just like it in front of her, supposedly to help settle her stomach, but she'd hardly touched it. They'd made the jump to hyperspace not long before, Lando walking Rinetta through what to do when he saw the condition of his cockpit.

"I'm going to let you handle that on your own," he said. "I need to change, anyway. We're about to be heroes, and I need to look the part."

So Rinetta and Zel had cleaned up the cockpit with no help from L3, who had her own mess to clean up. And now that her stomach was mostly settled, Rinetta decided that she never, ever wanted to be part of a Mustafarian Special again.

"I still don't understand why it's called a Mustafarian Special," Rinetta said.

"Because it's all fire and surprise," L3 responded, putting the last of the wipes she'd used to clean herself off in the refuse compartment. "Also because it ends badly for at least one side of the fight."

"Yeah, I don't get it," Rinetta said.

"You need to study more history," L3 said as she walked away.

"I thought it was funny," Zel said to no one in particular as she began to groom her ears.

"Nervous?" Rinetta asked, watching the Lynna.

"No. I am completing the largest quest in my planet's history. I'll be a hero," Zel said.

"You're scared," Rinetta said, seeing through her friend's boast.

"Yes," she mewled. "What if we are too late?"

"We won't be," Rinetta said. "I have a feeling about this."

But secretly, Rinetta was worried, as well. What if it wasn't really the Solstice Globe they carried with them in the cargo hold? Or worse, what if it was too late? What if they arrived to find the planet riddled with natural disasters? What if it had all been for nothing?

Rinetta straightened, giving herself a mental shake.

No. They would be fine. Everything was going to work out exactly right, because it had to. They had to save Livno, so they would.

They spent a couple of days on the *Millennium Falcon*. The trip through hyperspace was a long one, longer than Rinetta had ever taken, and there was nothing much to do while they waited.

That was how they ended up playing Sabacc.

"It's a simple game," Lando said as he shuffled the cards.

"Especially if you cheat," Zel said, ears laid back.

"Cheating is a matter of opinion," Lando smoothly corrected, a polite smile on his face. It seemed to Rinetta that Lando was always smiling, like it was just the natural arrangement of his face.

"As I was saying," Lando said, dealing cards around the table, "part of Sabacc is understanding the basic rules of the game. But the other part, the far more interesting part, is understanding how your opponents play the game. Do they embrace long odds or go for the sure thing?"

"Or do they cheat?" Zel growled.

"It's really only cheating if you get caught," L3 chimed in from a chair in the corner. She'd opted out of the game and instead had taken to oiling some of her couplings while everyone else played.

"Exactly, L3," Lando said. "Now, let's play."

Rinetta lost more hands than she won, but by the time she decided to lie down and get some rest, she knew more about Lando and the game of Sabacc than she would've thought possible.

Rinetta was in the middle of a dream about cantinas and smugglers when she jolted awake. They came out of hyperspace with a bump, and Rinetta got up, stretching and yawning. Zel sat nearby. "We're here," she said. It had been a couple of days since they'd left Hynestia, and Rinetta knew Zel had spent them worrying.

"Let's go get a look at your home planet," Rinetta told Zel, heading toward the cockpit.

Zel nodded. "There is no delaying this any longer, I fear."

When they got to the cockpit, L3 was nowhere to be found, but Lando was stretched out in his chair, stroking his mustache. "I have some questions," he said, gesturing at the space in front of them. Beyond lay an asteroid field, and Rinetta's heart sank.

"We're too late," she whispered.

"What's going on . . . ?" L3 asked, squeezing into the cockpit, pushing Rinetta and Zel to the side so she could sink into the copilot's seat.

"It happened. My planet has been destroyed," Zel said, ears lying flat. She sank into one of the jump seats, her shoulders slumped.

"What?" L3 said, leaning forward and fiddling with

some knobs. "No, this is just the remnant of a comet passing through. Hundred-year phenomenon. If we would've been a little bit earlier, we probably would've seen it." L3 made some adjustments, and the *Falcon* veered to the left, going around the debris field and revealing the first glimpse of Livno III. Rinetta held her breath. She'd waited so long for this.

"Anyway, there's your Livno III," L3 said.

The planet was covered in shades of purple, and lightning storms that could be seen from space battered the surface.

"We're going . . . there?" Lando said.

Zel stood up and leaned forward, ears swiveling with excitement as her trio of tails swished. Her normally gray stripes had gone happy pink. "Yes. We are going to my home."

"A promise is a promise," Rinetta said.

Lando sighed. "And so it is."

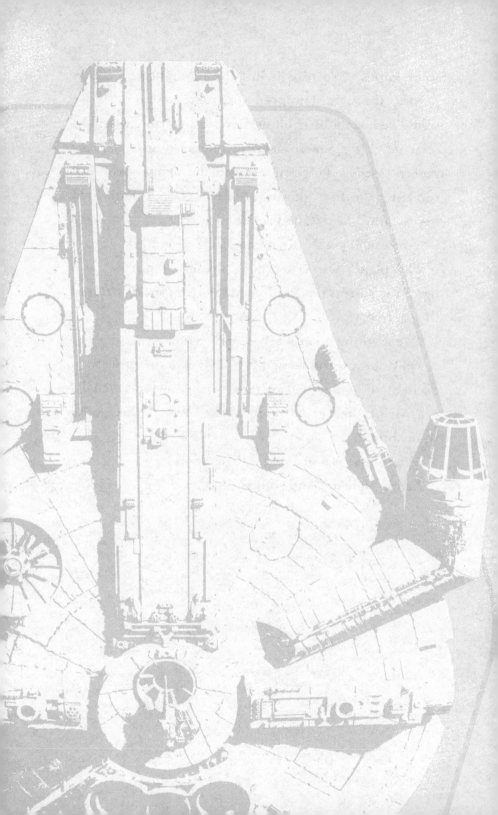

CHAPTER 20

Lando looked around the Chamber of the Sun and tried to put a value on all the jewels embedded in the walls. The large domed cavern they walked through had a hole at the highest point that revealed the sky, which was a stormy gray. The opening let in the wind and rain and enough light so the room sparkled in reds, greens, and blues. Some of the rocks he couldn't identify, but the ones he could made him grin in delight. Just a handful would clear all his debts. He surreptitiously pulled at one before Rinetta caught him and shook her head. He debated letting the rest of the group go ahead. Maybe he could go back to the *Millennium Falcon* and get a plasma torch to cut a few free. It wasn't like the Lynna would miss them. L3 pushed him from behind. "Not a good idea, Captain." Lando sighed.

Just his luck he would end up on the richest planet around and not get a chance to pocket any of the loot.

Zel pushed the crate carrying the Solstice Globe toward a grizzled old Lynna with solid-gray fur, his ears notched in a way that made them look vaguely wing-like. Zel had explained to them that meant he'd killed many in battle. The claws of his paws were curved and had been painted red, and Lando thought again about trying to pry loose a few jewels. Maybe not. He wasn't about to tempt the Lynna into showing just how he'd earned those notches. This was the first day in a while that no one had tried to kill Lando.

Still, he backed up to a wall and tugged, hoping at least one of the jewels would come free.

Nothing.

Lynna of all colors and ages gathered in the chamber behind the grizzled old Lynna, their eyes on Lando, Rinetta, Zel, and L3. Lando decided he should probably stop trying to pocket their jewels. It was bad manners to let someone catch you stealing from them.

There was a loud ringing, and as it faded away the grizzled old Lynna with the notched ears strode forward. "I am Zim Azul, leader of the free Lynna. I want to thank you, Lando Calrissian, Rinetta Gan, and Elthree-Three-Seven for returning our Solstice Globe to us," the ancient Lynna leader said in halting Basic.

Lando bowed his head respectfully, the same way Rinetta did. Oh well, if he couldn't be rich, he'd settle for being a legend.

"And thank you to our savior, Zel Gris, for returning our most sacred Solstice Globe. Zel, will you please do the honors?"

Zel looked at Rinetta, who gave a smile and encouraging nod. When Zel still hesitated, Lando grinned. "I could do it, if you'd rather." Lando imagined the Lynna carving his likeness into the cavern's jewel-covered surface. Heroes always got statues dedicated to them. It was a good thing he'd worn his best cape, the lime-green one lined tastefully with spotted hynax wool. He'd make a beautiful statue.

Zel hissed at him and opened the crate that held the Solstice Globe. Bright white light sliced through Lando's daydream and the chamber, and everyone covered their eyes as Zel removed the Solstice Globe from the crate. The orb was much smaller than Lando had imagined and fit comfortably in Zel's paws, where it glowed like a small sun.

"Oh," Rinetta breathed. "It's beautiful." Lando had to agree. No wonder it was priceless.

Zel carried it through the chamber to a spire in the middle of the room. The pointed column reminded Lando of a tree, and at the base of the trunk was an opening that already contained two other orbs that pulsed rhythmically. Lando couldn't tell what the thing was, but it was easy to see it held some kind of power.

Zel placed the Solstice Globe in the one remaining

spot, and there was a loud click. She stepped back to where the rest of the group stood, and they watched for a long moment.

"Is something supposed to happen?" Lando asked L3 in a low voice.

L3 shrugged. "How would I know? You think I just cruise through the galaxy, hanging out in strange and mysterious places so I can report back what I saw? I'm a navigator, not an info box."

"Is something supposed to happen?" Rinetta asked. Lando harrumphed. At least he wasn't the only one who'd been expecting *something*.

"We shall wait," Zim Azul said.

A sense of expectation filled the cavern, but still the rain and wind continued outside, occasional flashes of lightning visible through the opening in the top of the dome. Zel's tails swished in agitation, and her gray stripes shaded to a violet hue of distress. Rinetta shifted from foot to foot, and Lando wondered for a brief moment what the Lynna would do to them if it didn't work. He wasn't averse to fighting his way back to his ship, but he didn't want to mess up his best cape.

A deep humming came from the middle of Lando's chest, and before he could panic he realized it was actually coming from the chamber. The deep, droning buzz grew louder, and as it did the jewels in the walls began to glow, getting brighter and brighter until they began to flash in a pattern Lando didn't understand but thought was pretty nonetheless.

The Lynna began to murmur but were quickly drowned out by the building noise in the cavern. Just when Lando thought it couldn't get any louder, there was a boom, and a single beam of light shot out of the cavern, through the opening in the top of the dome and into the sky. It was too bright to look at for more than a few seconds, and Lando shielded his eyes, dazed.

"Well, that's something you don't see on Corellia," L3 said.

When Lando looked again, the spire's glow had faded to a rhythmic pulse, and the sky beyond the dome was a gentle lavender, the clouds quickly dispersing. Sunshine filtered down into the cavern, and a gentle breeze stirred the air.

"We did it," Rinetta said, a wide grin on her face. "We're heroes."

Lando felt the same kind of strange happiness. Rinetta had been right. Taking the Solstice Globe back to Livno III had been the right thing to do. If only doing the right thing didn't always mean being broke.

Oh, well.

"Livno III has been returned to its glory," Zim Azul announced to the gathered crowd. "And now, on this momentous occasion, we celebrate."

A cheer went up from the Lynna, and musical instruments began to appear. Platters of food were brought in from hidden doorways, and Lynna came over to congratulate Zel, Rinetta, L3, and Lando.

They really were heroes.

Still, Lando hoped there would be some kind of reward. He did have debts to cover.

CHAPTER 21

Hynestia looked so small from space. Rinetta watched as the planet grew bigger, nervousness churning her stomach. Not only had she directly defied her mother, she'd also stolen a valuable object from the Hynestian treasury and given it back to its rightful owners. It was something the earlier versions of her line never would have done. But she still believed it was the right thing to do.

She just had to convince the queen of that, as well.

Lando cleared his throat, and Rinetta drew her attention back to the cockpit and away from her own impending doom. "Are you sure I can't just drop you somewhere close by? A nice moon or something?"

Rinetta shook her head. "A promise—"

"—is a promise. Yeah, kid, I know. This is why I don't make promises. Because you fly to the edge of Wild Space and end up with nothing but a rock." Lando sighed. "Well, here's hoping your mom listens to our story before deciding to have me summarily executed."

Rinetta didn't say anything, just fingered the purple stone around her neck. Zel had said it would bring her luck, and it had. It had kept her safe and helped her accomplish her goals. Maybe it would help her navigate whatever came next.

The *Millennium Falcon* touched down in exactly the same spot it had left only days earlier. Rinetta's stomach growled. It hadn't been that long since she'd eaten, and yet she still felt hungry. Or maybe it was nervousness. She couldn't tell.

She missed Zel Gris. She really wished the Lynna were there with her blaster, ready to shoot anyone who threatened Rinetta.

Once the ship had landed and the boarding ramp had been lowered, Rinetta made her way to the cargo hold. She had only a few moments to wait before the Hynestian Royal Guard came running up the ramp, blasters raised menacingly.

"Lower your weapons," Rinetta said, trying for her best royal voice. A few of the guards hesitated, and Rinetta tried again. "Captain Calrissian and the droid are heroes. Lower your weapons!"

"First mate," L3-37 corrected. "Not droid, first mate."

"You are correct. My apologies. First mate and the best navigator in the known galaxy."

L3 crossed her arms. "Much better."

Rinetta had to fight to keep the smile off her face, and instead gave the guards her best glare.

They lowered their weapons.

"Rinetta." The queen stood in the entryway to the hangar, her expression torn between anger and relief.

"Hi, Mom," Rinetta said, dropping all formality for a moment. She was so happy to see her mother that tears threatened to spring forth, but she squared her shoulders and drew herself up. "Exalted Mother, I have returned."

Her words must have reminded the queen where she was, because she gave herself a little shake and strode over to where Rinetta stood in the entryway to the *Falcon*.

"Princess Rinetta, what is the meaning of this?" Queen Forsythia wasn't wearing her normal formal attire. Instead, she wore her training garb, a blaster slung low on her hip. She'd thrown a purple gherlian cloak over her shoulders in her haste to get to the hangar, and the color made Rinetta a little sad. Purple was the color for battle, but it was also the color of mourning. Had the queen thought Rinetta was dead? Or had she been preparing to come after the *Falcon*?

Guilt washed over Rinetta. She'd been so focused on doing the right thing that she hadn't considered how her sudden disappearance would affect her mother. Sure, everyone might know the queen as terrifying and stately, but Rinetta also knew her as the one person in the galaxy who loved her more than anything else. She was the one who had taught her how to make good decisions and how to pursue her goals.

So she should understand better than anyone else why Rinetta had done what she'd done.

She took a deep breath. "Exalted Mother, I have returned the payment due to the Empire. Captain Calrissian and his first mate," Rinetta said, gesturing to indicate L3, "informed me of a plan to offload the gherlian furs on Neral's moon, and Captain Calrissian agreed to help me stop the thieves and return the cargo."

"He did?" Queen Forsythia said, her doubt obvious.

"He did," Rinetta said, daring Lando to contradict her story.

"I did. But unfortunately, the gherlian thieves got away," he said.

"Which is why we used the Solstice Globe as bait to lure them to the Black Spire Outpost on Batuu. And once they were there and we made certain they had the furs, we took care of the problem," Rinetta announced.

"And how, exactly, did you find these criminals?" Captain Twyla asked. "We've been looking for that cargo for weeks."

"Oh, Captain Calrissian has a number of shady contacts," Rinetta said matter-of-factly.

"Hey, I just happen to know a lot of enterprising folks," Lando said.

"Soooo many shady contacts," L3 chimed in. "Veritable forest of ne'er-do-wells."

Rinetta went to the compartment and knocked on it three times like she'd seen L3 do her first day on the *Falcon*. A panel fell away, and the furs came tumbling out.

Lucky for Rinetta, the exclamations of surprise covered up Lando's groan of disappointment.

"Guards, seize our cargo," Queen Forsythia said, and the guards hurried to collect the gherlian furs and seal them up in a new container. "And what of the orb?"

"It was destroyed in the firefight," Rinetta said. "It made a delightful explosion."

Queen Forsythia sighed. "Well. We suppose there must be sacrifices. The furs are worth much more, so thank you, honored daughter." And lower, so only Rinetta could hear: "I am glad you are home, heart of my heart."

"I missed you, too, Momma," Rinetta said in a similarly low voice.

They all watched from outside the *Falcon* as the guards unloaded the furs until one of them came back with the pretty sparkly rock Zel had given Lando. "Should we take this, as well?"

"Might as well. Why not take the seats while you're at it?" Lando said.

"That's Lando's lucky rock," Rinetta said, shaking her head. "That was gifted to him by Zel Gris after Lando saved her life. I got one, too. Also, Zel agreed to help us if we commuted her sentence."

"Yes, we cannot help but notice that you also freed your friend. There is no reason a princess should override a queen's command," Queen Forsythia said, her expression hardening.

Rinetta's good cheer melted away, and her heart began to pound. She wanted her mother to be proud of her, but letting Zel go had also been the right thing to do, especially since it was Rinetta who had planned to steal the Solstice Globe from the treasury.

Rinetta opened her mouth to confess the whole miserable truth, but before she did the queen spoke. "But loyalty is to be admired. It is a rare trait indeed in these fraught times. You have done well, Exalted Daughter," Queen Forsythia said.

Rinetta bowed. "Thank you, Exalted Mother."

"Please give Captain Calrissian back his rock," Queen Forsythia said.

Lando grabbed his sparkly rock from the guard and tucked it under his arm. "Thank you."

"Do you mind if I see that for a moment?" Queen Forsythia asked, a frown creasing the brown skin of her forehead.

Lando shrugged. "I don't see why not. It's just a pretty space rock."

After a brief examination Queen Forsythia raised a

single eyebrow at Lando and handed the rock back to him. "Captain Calrissian, that pretty space rock, as you so casually called it, is very expensive. It's pure kakaorzum, a highly coveted element. The Lynna gave you a very valuable gift."

Lando looked down at his rock and grinned. "Well, I'll be."

"It does strike us that there should be a fine for your previous smuggling infraction," the queen said. Lando's smile evaporated.

"Exalted, we have the entire shipment of gherlian furs," Captain Twyla said.

Queen Forsythia smiled. "But we have already been blessed with an abundance of fortune today. So enjoy your rock."

Lando let out a deep breath.

Captain Twyla cleared her throat. "There is some other contraband within the compartments, but it doesn't belong to us."

"And we will not borrow trouble. Thank you, Captain Twyla," Queen Forsythia said. "And with that, we ask that you and the droid—excuse us, your first mate—leave our planet. And never, ever return," Queen Forsythia said. She wasn't smiling, but her light tone made Rinetta think that maybe even her mother had gotten something out of this entire misadventure.

Lando didn't have to be told twice. He dipped his

head in respect and gave a final jaunty salute. "Queen Forsythia, Princess. Good luck." He made his way back up the boarding ramp, L3 right behind him.

As the ramp rose, Rinetta sighed. "Do you think we'll see Captain Calrissian and the *Millennium Falcon* again?"

"We certainly hope not. That is a man who cannot help but attract trouble, no matter what he does."

Rinetta walked out of the hangar with her mother and the retinue of guards, her own rock of kakaorzum heavy in her pocket. The royal speeder was waiting for them outside of the hangar, and already guards were taking the purloined gherlian furs to be packed off to the Empire. Their annual payment would arrive just in time, but what about next year, or the year after that? What if the Empire decided the furs were no longer sufficient? What then?

Rinetta looked up as the *Millennium Falcon* lifted out of the hangar, streaking across the sky with a blued light as it headed to space and Calrissian's next misadventure. Rinetta was no gambler, but she would lay odds that he was off to his next Sabacc game, off to his next load of goods to smuggle. Maybe one day he would even get to live the life of a sportsman, as he'd said he wanted to.

Lando Calrissian was living his best life, and one day she would, too.

Bazine Netal leaned back in her seat and blinked. "That's some story."

"And a story is what you paid me for," the woman said, standing with a smile. "And now, if you don't mind, I will be on my way."

"Wait, I have more questions," Bazine said. She wanted to know more about the capabilities of the ship, which modifications were there when the woman was on the *Millennium Falcon*. Not just some woman. Princess Rinetta of Hynestia—the Lost Princess as she was sometimes known throughout the galaxy. Bazine had heard the stories. Everyone had. When Queen Forsythia lost her planet to the Empire, she hadn't gone quietly, fighting to the bitter end. But by the time the Empire claimed the planet, there was little left: a few burned-out domes where gherlian fur had once grown, an underground city overrun with feral reptiles that could swallow a man with a single bite, and a hologram of the queen telling the Empire exactly what she thought of it. But not a single Hynestian had been found. They'd all disappeared.

The queen had ended up on Neral's moon, where she died an old woman, completely anonymous until after her death, when a maid recognized her.

Warships searched that sector of space for months, looking for the royal family and any Hynestians. But not a single one could be found. It was thought that maybe only Queen Forsythia had survived. She was, after all, known for being an assassin. It was how she'd gained her throne.

But looking at the old woman across from her, Bazine thought she knew what had happened to the Hynestians. They'd fled to Livno III, wherever that was, and Bazine wanted to know more about that rich, undiscovered planet filled with kakaorzum. It wasn't the intelligence she had been looking for, but all information was valuable.

"I'm sorry. That's all I have for you," Rinetta said. The pendant around her neck had come loose from her cloak, and the pretty purple rock swung back and forth alluringly.

"Perhaps you could tell me how to get to Livno III?" Bazine asked, wondering what she could use to make the old woman talk. What kinds of powders did she have at her disposal? She could slip a little into the woman's drink, make the taking of the information easier. "Perhaps I can get you another glass of juice?"

"I don't think so. And surely you must know, my dear, that Livno III isn't the planet's real name? The name of the place we went has been lost to history, and that is exactly how the Lynna like it."

"I just need to know what the ship contained. Weapons, engines—" A loud slam distracted Bazine. Just a moment, a glance at the door, and when Bazine turned back to where the old woman had been, she was gone.

"No," Bazine breathed. She was the best. And she was the best because she was careful.

But for some reason, that woman had made her feel comfortable. Safe.

Comfort was deadly.

Bazine ran out the front entrance. The deserted street gave her no clues, only muddy boots, and running back into the cantina revealed only the same scene she'd left. The old woman was gone. There wasn't even a speck of dirt on the stone floor to reveal her passing.

"Very well played, Princess," Bazine murmured, crossing her arms.

Still, she had more information about the *Millennium Falcon* than she'd had when she began.

Bazine would find out all she could about this Corellian freighter. Because she was the best.

Beeping came across Bazine's private comlink channel. "Yes," she said.

"You're looking for a ship," came a raspy voice.

"I am. You have information?"

"I do," the unidentified caller said. "For a price. Two hundred credits."

"Done," Bazine said. The voice gave her an account number, and she sent the money.

"Excellent. Your ship. I heard that some Weequay pirate who's always prattling on about besting a Jedi has that ship. You can find him on Batuu. Black Spire Outpost."

The connection dropped, and Bazine tapped a Rishi ink–stained fingertip against the side of her head as she thought. Batuu was a long way from Vixnix, and it would take a while to get there. But after hearing Rinetta's story, Bazine was even more determined to find the *Millennium Falcon*. Nothing would stop her.

The ship couldn't hide forever.

Justina Ireland lives with her husband, kid, cat, and dog in Pennsylvania. She is the author of *Vengeance Bound*, *Promise of Shadows*, and *Dread Nation*, a *New York Times* best seller. You can visit her on Twitter as @justinaireland, on Instagram as @justinai, or at her website justinaireland.com.

Annie Wu is an illustrator currently living in Chicago. She is best known for her work in comics, including DC's Black Canary and Marvel's Hawkeye. Her previous work for *Star Wars* includes the Join the Resistance series by Ben Acker & Ben Blacker.

A
Great
Stone
Face
Book!

Mayfield Crossing

Mayfield Crossing

VAUNDA MICHEAUX NELSON

with illustrations by
Leonard Jenkins

G. P. PUTNAM'S SONS *New York*

G. P. Putnam's Sons, a division of The Putnam & Grosset Group,
200 Madison Avenue, New York, NY 10016.
Published simultaneously in Canada.
Printed in the United States of America.
Designed by Patrick Collins.
Text set in Palatino.

Library of Congress Cataloging-in-Publication Data
Nelson, Vaunda Micheaux.
Mayfield Crossing / by Vaunda Micheaux Nelson.   p.   cm.
Summary: When the school in Mayfield Crossing is closed,
the students are sent to larger schools, where the black children
encounter racial prejudice for the first time. Only baseball
seems a possibility for drawing people together.
[1. Race relations—Fiction.   2. Prejudices—Fiction.   3. Schools—
Fiction.   4. Baseball—Fiction.]   I. Title.
PZ7.N43773 May   1992   [Fic]—dc20   92-10564   CIP   AC
ISBN 0-399-22331-2

10 9 8 7 6

For Olive Batch Micheaux
and Norris Edward Micheaux, Jr.,
my mother and father

Mayfield Crossing

Prologue

Papa once said being different is both a blessing and a curse. He said people who are different give ordinary people something to talk about so they don't get bored with having to live with themselves all the time. I laughed at that, and so did Billie and Mama. Then he said that people who are different make things happen; they change things.

"What if people like things the way they are?" I asked.

Papa's forehead wrinkled as he lowered his eyebrows and said, "That's when the blessing becomes a curse."

He didn't say more about it, and I never asked him to explain. But since then, I've been finding out for myself—the bad and the good.

I suppose it really started a long time ago, with Harry. But I didn't begin to understand until last September. The day Dillon's father brought home their brand-new 1960 Studebaker. The day we played our last ball game together before things changed.

❧ *Chapter One*

It was hot and dusty, and the woods that surrounded the Crossing were still mostly green, but some of the trees were touched with red or orange or yellow. I hadn't seen much beyond those woods and the town of Mayfield Crossing, none of us had.

Tomorrow we will, I thought, catching a perfect pitch.

"Strike two," I said, keeping the cool in my voice but feeling like jumping clean to the sky, both for the strike and for tomorrow.

Billie didn't even crack a smile. He knew the game wasn't over. He was concentrating on his next pitch.

My brother had some arm. He could throw a ball so hard it stung your hand right through the mitt. We needed a pitch like that now. The score was tied at six, they had runners on second and third, there were two outs, and Luke Cleary was up.

I slid my catcher's mask away from my face.

"Keep it on, Meg," Billie called in his protective way.

"Can't see," I yelled back, but flipped it down just the same.

"You're doin' fine," Luke said, taking a practice swing, his red hair reflecting the sunlight. "That was a good call. I shoulda swung."

That meant something, coming from Luke. He was eleven, two years older, and treating me like an equal. Luke was good. Real good. Most times, if he was on your team, you could plan on winning.

But we were lucky today. We had Fitch Sherman on our side. He was the king of double plays and loved playing shortstop, but, as usual, we only had four players on each team, so today he was covering between first and second base. His twin brother Owen was covering second and third. From where I was, it was like seeing double.

Owen was the fastest talker this side of the tracks, but he couldn't play baseball worth spit. Trouble was, Owen stuck to his brother like glue. It was common knowledge in Mayfield Crossing that if you planned anything with Fitch, you got the whole package. But Owen was all right. I'd eat a plateful of liver if I ever heard he told a lie.

"Take your time, Turner. Take your time," Owen called to Billie.

Dillon Wood was standing on the tree stump we used as second base, looking the other way, probably bird-

watching. He was the best on foot in the Crossing, famous for stretching a double or even a triple out of a hit that'd only put most on first base. But it was Alice Cleary I was worried about.

She had her foot right on the edge of our third-base rock, ready to charge the instant Luke connected or I dropped a ball. Alice could steal a base fast as a jack rabbit, and she was known for blinding the catcher with dust on a slide. It hadn't rained in weeks, so already the dust was heavy, showing like powder on my brown arms. I tugged one of my pigtails, then threw it behind my shoulder. I knew I could catch, but I wasn't good under pressure.

"Come on, Lukey," Mo Cleary said from behind me. She was up next and standing on a log near home plate. Right then, I wished it was her on third base instead of Alice. Mo never stole a base in her life. Didn't think it was fair.

If Luke struck out, it would be the bottom of the ninth and our chance to break the tie and win the game. With school starting tomorrow, it would be the last game of the summer, so everybody wanted to win bad. A cloudburst with lightning and thunder couldn't have ended the game.

Luke held the bat like he planned to send the ball to Jupiter. But just as Billie threw his emergency pitch, a

slow curve ball we called the "Untouchable Turner," Dillon shouted, "Here comes Old Hairy!"

"Shoot," Billie said.

Luke dropped the bat and ran toward left field.

By the time I knew what had happened, the ball was safe in my glove and everybody was running. Running away from the dusty Mayfield School ball field, away from the game of the year, maybe the best short-handed game of our entire lives. But nobody cared who won anymore.

"Come on, Meg!" Billie yelled.

I picked up the bat and raced over third base after them. We all hid behind some bushes and, catching my breath, I watched Old Hairy come out of the woods behind first base and stroll onto the field.

Old Hairy wasn't really that old, but he was strange. He wore faded overalls and a plaid flannel shirt even though it was hot as blazes. And he had so many whiskers, he looked like a werewolf. Mama said he was "an original." But to Mayfield kids, he was a terror.

Old Hairy skipped up to home plate with a quick, light step, kind of like he was doing a soft-shoe dance. He moved his arms like he was swinging a bat, then started running around the bases.

"Man, he's crazy," Owen said.

"Yeah," Billie said, wiping sweat from his forehead

with his shirttail and keeping his eyes on Hairy, "but at least Old Hairy won't be crashing our games at the new school. He won't be able to find us."

I glanced across the field at the Mayfield schoolhouse. It was a sorry sight with the windows all boarded up. Tomorrow we were going to Parkview Elementary, a bigger school with kids from other neighborhoods. It had been nice, being in a small school, knowing everybody. But we'd heard that Parkview had a huge ball field with thick grass, and we were itching to try it out. And there would be lots more kids, so we'd be sure to have enough players to cover the field. Besides, at Mayfield Old Hairy was always coming around and breaking things up. We'd be safe from him at Parkview.

A loud whistle pierced the air. It was Mrs. Sherman calling for the twins.

"I'm not leavin' these bushes," Owen said. "Not 'til Old Hairy's outta here."

Mama'd be calling us in soon, too, and she'd be sore if we were late for supper because of Hairy.

She was funny about Old Hairy. She got mad at us for running away from him. I wondered if she'd think differently if she knew what we knew about Hairy—and about his hatchet.

We all stood closer together. I tugged my pigtail and hoped those years of Sunday School would pay off, but

my mind was blank. I couldn't seem to remember even one of the hundreds of prayers I'd learned. I whispered "Amen" anyway, just in case *wanting* to say a prayer was as good as doing it and the Lord would come through after all.

As Hairy rounded third base and came past our hiding place, everybody ducked back behind the bushes. But I wasn't quick enough. Old Hairy looked dead at me and held his hand up. Mama would have wanted me to wave back, but I couldn't.

Luke pulled me down out of sight, then we all peeked out again, just as Hairy was running across home plate.

"Jeepers, I didn't know he could move like *that*," Luke whispered.

"He's pretty fast all right," I said, wondering if I could outrun him if I had to.

❧ *Chapter Two*

"We should've won by default," Alice insisted, standing on our back porch after supper, one hand on her hip. She combed the fingers of her other hand through her tangled red hair and said, "Our team was still willing to play." Alice was a serious player. She got real mad when things didn't go her way. But we understood. There are times when a person can't be held responsible.

"Come on, Alice," Mo said, her freckled hands folded on top of her head. "That wouldn't be right. Most of Billie's team had to leave. It could have been any of us called home."

"It was an even game," Billie said. He was sitting on the porch floor, his big, dark eyes—eyes like Papa's—focused on a rip in the knee of his overalls.

"Maybe," Alice went on. "But if it hadn't been for Old Hairy, we'd have whipped your tails."

"No way," Owen protested. "Billie was just about to strike out Luke the Duke."

Luke started to take his glasses off like he does when he's about to convince you of something.

But before he could, I cut in, "Nobody knows what would've happened."

"Right," Mo agreed. "Like Billie said, it was an even game."

Finally Alice plopped into a chair. "Okay. Okay. But we're gonna whip the tails off those Parkview kids when we play them."

Everybody laughed. Kids from the Crossing didn't fight much. Not for real. And when they did, the mad didn't stick.

"I wish he'd get here," Dillon said from the porch step. I don't think he'd heard a word about the game. He was waiting for his dad. The two of them were real close. He didn't have a mom. She died when he was five.

Today Mr. Wood was bringing home his first new car. It was a big deal for all of us. We were used to second-hand.

"Well, is it time yet?" Luke asked.

Dillon didn't answer. He strained his neck to see down the narrow blacktop road that crossed the railroad tracks. His yellow cowlick was standing up so straight it looked like it was straining to see, too. It would have been easier

to watch from the front porch, but after Old Hairy showed up there one day last spring, we felt safer out back.

"Is it time yet?" Luke asked again.

"No," Dillon finally said. "Still, I wish he'd come."

We laughed. But I knew what he meant. Waiting is hard, whether it's for something bad like a report card, or something good like Christmas, or even something like going to Parkview School.

"I can't wait 'til tomorrow!" I blurted out. "Mama made me a new dress. It's blue plaid with a white collar."

"Grandma made dresses for Alice and me, too." Mo was excited. "The one I'm wearing tomorrow is green. Gram says I look good in green."

"I hate 'em," said Alice. "They're all frilly and starch-scratchy, like church clothes. How're we gonna play ball?"

"Billie's gonna wear a tie," I teased, nudging him with my elbow, hoping to get him riled.

"Am not." Billie flashed a look at me, then glanced around at everybody else. "Papa said other boys probably won't wear them and I might feel out of place. So Mama changed her mind."

"Our mom said there might be some people at Parkview who don't want us there, so there might be some trouble," Fitch said in a low voice. His eyes were serious. He and Owen had the same gray eyes and tight curls of

black hair. But up close, it was easy to tell who was who.

"What kind of trouble?" I asked.

Fitch folded his arms in front of him. "I don't know, but Pop told us to mind our p's and q's, whatever that means."

"I guess we can do whatever we want to with the rest of the alphabet," Owen said, grinning.

That Owen. Fitch pretended to push him over the porch rail.

"I'm just glad we'll all be at the same school." Mo put her arm behind me on the porch swing.

When Mayfield School closed, some politicians divided the Crossing into north, south, east, and west sections and spread us around to different schools. Some kids were going to Liberty, Washington, or Riverside School. We were the east section and going to Parkview.

"What if they had drawn the dividing line right between our houses?" Mo said.

"I would have died!" I cried, hugging her closer.

Beep, beep!

"He's here!" Dillon said, so quiet I hardly heard. He practically flew off the steps, and we all charged after him.

Mr. Wood was waving out the car window as he pulled up in a shiny, willow-green station wagon. A 1960 Studebaker Lark. It was a clumsy-looking car with a sort of a fish-mouth grill. We had had wild dreams of a Lincoln

Continental with the "suicide" back doors that opened from the wrong end. But nobody was complaining about the Studebaker. It was the nicest car any of us had ever seen, except in pictures or from a distance.

"Ooooweee!" Dillon exclaimed, running around and around the car.

"I can see myself," Alice said, looking at her reflection in the chrome bumper.

"A star of a car," Owen sang.

"Can we have a ride?" Dillon asked, leaning in the window on the passenger side.

Mr. Wood smiled and said, "Sure, if it's all right with everyone's folks."

By now, our folks had heard the commotion and were gathering around the car.

"Nice," Papa said, nodding his head. "Nice."

Mama wiped her hands on her checked apron. Then she came over, reached in a window, and felt the soft green seats. "Mmmmm," she said, like she had tasted something real good.

"Can we? Can we go for a ride?" I begged, jumping up and down.

Billie looked up at Mama, his face asking the same thing.

She put her hand on top of my head to stop my jumping. "All right," she said, laughing, "but tomorrow is

school, so when you get back, it's into the tub with both of you, then early to bed. Deal?"

"Deal!" Billie and I said together.

"But Meg first!" Billie added, running to get into the car. On a regular night, I might have argued, but tonight I was feeling so good I didn't care. Besides, I figured now I'd have something to bargain with on another night.

Everybody was allowed to go, but first, even though we'd already dusted each other off after the ball game, Mr. Wood made us do it again. Dust was flying everywhere, like when Mama beat rugs she'd hung over the clothesline.

Dillon sat up front with Alice. Fitch, Owen, and Billie got in the back seat. And Mo and I climbed into the wayback. As we pulled away, I heard Mrs. Cleary holler, "Can we have a turn tomorrow?"

"If the kids say it's okay," Mr. Wood called back, and we drove off down the road.

I'll remember that car ride until the day I die. The Crossing passed by the window—Mason's Drug Store, the Five and Ten, Keegan's Gas Station, the Dairy Queen. The radio blared "You Ain't Nothin' But a Hound Dog," with all of us singing like Elvis. And the smell . . . the smell was all newness.

✿ *Chapter Three*

It was me driving that car in my mind when Mama and Papa came to tuck us in.

Papa sat on Billie's bed and Mama sat on mine. "You two go right off to sleep now," Mama said, kissing both my cheeks. "No talking after lights out. You have a big day tomorrow."

Papa said something to Billie that I couldn't hear. Then he looked over and said, "Meg, remember you might not get to sit near Mo in your class tomorrow. If that happens, try to see it as a chance to get to know the other children, to make new friends."

"Yes, Papa."

Both he and Mama were quiet for a while. I could tell there was something else they wanted to say. I turned onto my side and pulled my knees up close to my chest.

"Mama," I said, breaking the silence. "Mrs. Sherman

told Fitch and Owen that some people at Parkview might not want us there. She said there could be trouble. Is that true?"

Mama looked over at Papa. "It's possible," she said. "Some people are uncomfortable with folks they don't know. Folks who may be a little different from them."

"You mean 'cause we're from Mayfield?"

"Partly, yes," Papa said, "but you may be the only Negro in your class. Billie, too."

So what? I wanted to say.

I was glad that, just then, Mama smiled and said, "You just be as friendly and polite as you can be and things will be fine." She patted my behind and walked over to kiss Billie. Papa leaned over my bed. I put my arms around his neck, and he kissed me on my nose.

"Lights out now," he said, flicking the switch.

After they left, I whispered, "What did Papa say to you?"

"He told me to look out for you," Billie said and turned to face the wall.

Papa didn't have to say that. Billie would look after me anyway. Besides, I could take care of myself. And how could there be trouble? They were just kids, like us. I turned over and wished for morning, when I could put on my new plaid dress with the crisp white collar.

* * *

17

In the morning, Mama and Papa didn't say anything else about trouble. Before Papa left for work, he just said, "You have a good day, now." I figured they had talked last night and decided there wasn't anything to worry about.

I felt like a queen in my new dress, and was in heaven when Mama cut two pieces of blue ribbon for the ends of my pigtails. "I don't know why I bother with these," she sighed, tying them on. "They'll be lost by the end of the day." She was probably right. That's why she put rubber bands on underneath. But I decided to try real hard to make it through the whole day with both bows.

Before we left, Mama stood Billie and me in front of a mirror in the dining room and said, "You two look so grown up." She sounded a little sad.

Billie smiled, proud. He did look older, taller, and I was almost as tall as him. Mama was tall for a woman, people said. I guess I got it from her. Billie was wearing gray pants and a light blue shirt. Our clothes sort of matched, but I would never say so. Billie'd have a fit.

On my way out the front door, I remembered to peek out through the screen to check for Old Hairy. If there was going to be any trouble, I figured it would come from him, not Parkview folks. The coast was clear.

At the bus stop, Mo spun around to show me her dress. It was glorious, with a green hair ribbon to match.

"Wow! The ribbon goes with your eyes," I said, then showed her mine.

Alice had on a red and gray striped jumper with a white blouse. She kept tugging at her collar, but she looked good.

Fitch and Owen both had on brown pants, but different shirts. They never dressed exactly alike, like some twins. Mr. and Mrs. Sherman said they wanted Fitch and Owen to grow up to be two people, not one.

Everybody looked real nice in their first-day clothes. Even Dillon's cowlick was slicked down and staying— until about lunch time, I figured.

"Think there'll be a ball game at recess on the first day?" Luke asked. "I brought my glove. Did you?"

Everybody had.

"I didn't bring the bat," Billie said. "There'll probably be one at Parkview."

"We're lucky we even *have* a bat after yesterday," Fitch said loudly. Then he turned to Luke, teasing. "Hey, how come Meg risked her neck to save our bat from Old Hairy and all you could do was save yourself?"

The bat belonged to everybody. We'd all chipped in the summer before, after Billie's and then Luke's bat had been broken. We took turns keeping it at home.

"Yeah, Cleary," Billie joined in. "I think my little sister must have more guts than you."

I didn't like being called little, but I couldn't help smiling. I don't know what made me stop for the bat. I was as scared of Hairy as everybody else.

Luke flapped his arms and clucked like a chicken. Then he punched me lightly on the shoulder and said, "That *was* pretty cool, Meg."

He and Alice boosted me up on Billie's shoulders like they do to heroes. I felt like a million bucks.

❧ Chapter Four

The woods and twisty roads of Mayfield soon disappeared behind us as the school bus turned onto streets lined with sidewalks and new brick houses with grass so perfect it didn't look real. Parkview School was big and new and crowded with kids, all talking at once. Some were staring as we got off the bus, or pointing and saying that we were "the new kids from Mayfield."

"See you at lunch," Alice said as she went off with Fitch and Owen to the fifth grade.

While Luke and Dillon were looking for the sixth-grade rooms, Billie squeezed my shoulder and asked, "You gonna be okay?"

Most times, I liked the way he looked after me, but I was in the fourth grade now and ready to take care of myself. I didn't want to hurt his feelings, so I just gave him the thumbs up sign, grabbed Mo's arm, and headed down the hall.

"If you need me, I'll be in Room 6A," he called after me.

"Okay," I said without looking back.

When we got to our classroom, there were name cards on each desk so we'd know where the teacher wanted us to sit. I looked at Mo's face three rows away and could see she was as disappointed as I was.

It was just like Papa said. But I also remembered he had said to try to see it as a chance to make new friends, so I decided to make the best of it.

As the desks filled up, I realized that Papa had been right about something else, too. I was the only Negro in the class. I still didn't understand why Papa seemed so worried about it. There hadn't been many Negroes at Mayfield either—Billie and me, the Shermans, and a few others—and we never had trouble with the kids there.

But Papa had said, "Every place isn't like the Crossing. Mayfield is special." I looked over at Mo. Not counting family, I was closer to her than anybody.

I glanced at the girl with short blonde hair seated across the aisle. She didn't see me. I read her name card—IVY SCOTT. Ivy. She reminded me of Dillon without the cowlick. From what I could see, her eyes were blue like his, too.

A boy wearing thick glasses and a shirt that looked real starched was in the seat behind her. When he leaned forward to say something to Ivy, his hand covered his name card.

I was trying to see the name of the girl with brown curls in front of me when the boy behind me pulled my pigtail. It didn't really hurt, and kids at Mayfield did that all the time, mostly if they liked you. I turned around and smiled at a head of straight black hair. He was looking in the other direction, like it was somebody else who'd done it. CLAYTON REED, his card said. He looked big for a fourth grader. The teacher started talking just then, so I faced the front.

"Welcome to Parkview School," the man said, adjusting his glasses. "I'm Mr. Stanley, and I hope you're all as excited as I am to be here." He looked real young for a teacher, younger than Papa.

"The beginning of a school year always offers new possibilities," he said, "a fresh start on things. But this is an extra special year for Parkview."

Mr. Stanley had a friendly face, but he seemed nervous. Like he might not remember all of the speech he'd prepared.

"Some new students have entered our school. Students from a little town called Mayfield Crossing."

Some kids looked around at me. I glanced over at Mo and saw kids had turned and looked at her, too.

"They will feel a bit uncomfortable at first. Everyone does in a new place." Mr. Stanley walked down Mo's aisle. "But the rest of us can do a lot to help the new students in this class, and throughout the school, feel welcome."

He put his hand on top of a boy's head and turned it away from Mo. Other kids who had been staring turned to face the front.

"There's a lot we can learn from each other," Mr. Stanley said.

It sounded so much like something Papa might say that I was beginning to feel right at home.

It was great to see the rest of the gang at lunchtime. Only six people fit at a table, and Mo and I were the last to arrive, so we said hello to everybody and took the nearest seats we could find at a table with some Parkview kids.

"Hi," I said as we sat down. "I'm Meg Turner and this is . . ."

Before I could finish, all four kids picked up their lunches and, without a word, got up and left.

"Hey, what's . . . ?" I started to say, but they were gone.

"Maybe they're in fifth or sixth grade," Mo said. "A girl told me this morning that the big kids here don't like to hang around with the littler kids."

I strained to get a better look at them as they sat down a few tables away. They didn't look that old to me.

"That doesn't make any sense at all," I said.

I caught Billie's eye, and he came over.

"What happened with those kids?" he asked.

By the time Mo had finished telling it, Luke, Alice, Dillon, and the twins had come over, too.

"You guys aren't going to stop talking to us, are you, just 'cause you're older?" Mo asked.

"Don't be dumb," Luke said. He spit in his hand. We all did the same, then joined in one big handshake, and swore that we'd stay friends.

Mo was sure those kids left because we were fourth graders, but later, at recess, we all found out different.

A big kid from Parkview called, "Game!" and everybody headed down toward the ball field to pick up teams. This was what we'd been waiting for. We grabbed our ball gloves and followed the other kids down toward the chain-link backstop behind home plate.

Billie and Luke figured they wouldn't get to be captains right off, seeing that they were new.

"Maybe not," I said, poking Billie, "but wait 'til they come up against the Untouchable Turner."

"Luke the Duke is gonna clean up," Owen said. "And Fitch'll hang 'em out to dry, iron 'em, and stack 'em in neat little piles."

"Yeah? And what are you gonna do, Owen?" Alice said, laughing.

For the first time in his life Owen surprised us all.

"I'm gonna sit this first one out," he said. "I wanna check out the new players."

26

He sounded cool saying it, but there was something else in his voice, something unsure. I tugged my pigtail. Fitch playing ball with Owen on the sidelines? It wouldn't seem right. Fitch put his arm around Owen's neck as we walked along.

The two Parkview team captains were a sixth grader named Judd, and Clayton, that boy who'd pulled my pigtail. They did the hand-over-hand on the bat, same as we did, to decide who got first pick. Judd won, and right away he pointed to a blond boy standing next to him.

"Cool!" the boy said.

Clayton chose a large boy with a crew cut and ears that stuck out.

Next Judd picked a short kid. The boy ran over punching the pocket of his glove. He looked a lot like Judd, so I thought they might be brothers. It was nice of Judd to choose him. Like Fitch would do with Owen.

Then Clayton picked Ivy Scott. She was wearing a nice red jumper with a white blouse and carrying a mitt that looked all oiled and broken in. She bent over and started tying on Keds she had brought. I was impressed and wondered if Mama would let me bring mine. I could see Alice was thinking the same thing. Only she'd probably rather just wear hers—even with a skirt.

Judd chose again. Then Clayton, and by the time it was over all of us Mayfield kids were still standing there

without a team. They hadn't even picked Billie or Luke, who were sixth graders. The Parkview kids didn't speak to any of us, or even look at us. Just acted like we didn't exist, like we weren't even taking up space on the planet.

Alice was hot. We all were. But she was the one who lost it.

"Hey!" she hollered. "This ain't right. Don't you know that when you pick up a game, everybody who shows up gets to play? Even if you don't know how good they are? Even if they're not that good?"

"Cool it, Alice," Luke said. "Yelling won't help."

The Parkview kids just started playing their game, still not saying anything to us.

I could tell Billie was as mad as Alice, but he didn't say a word. He just jerked his head to the side, signaling us all to come away from the game. "This field doesn't belong to them," Alice was saying as Luke and Dillon pulled her along with us. "We go to this school now, too, and they're gonna have to learn to share it whether they like it or not." She was so mad she was almost crying.

"You're right," Mo said. "But Luke's right too. Yelling at them won't do any good."

We walked over toward the playground and stopped at the swings. The swings at Mayfield had had wooden seats, worn smooth from years of kids riding. These were a new kind with rubber slings that squeezed together

when you sat down. Bum pinchers. I didn't like them. I don't think the rest of the gang did either, but nobody said anything.

I tugged my pigtail and felt only the rubber band holding my hair together. The other ribbon was still there, but hanging untied, like it was too tired to be a bow anymore.

I looked back toward the game. Everything we'd heard about Parkview's ball field was true. It was neat and green and the diamond seemed almost like the ones they had in the big leagues. But just then, I missed Mayfield's dusty, rocky field so much my stomach hurt.

❧ *Chapter Five*

"You shoulda seen the way they treated us," I told Mama and Papa after school. "It was like we were nothin'."

"Worse than that," Billie mumbled. He had been quiet the whole way on the bus coming home.

Mama poured us each a tall glass of milk and allowed us two chocolate-chip cookies. They were still warm and were loaded with walnuts. She hardly ever let us have sweets before supper. Even Billie started to perk up a little.

"Give it time," Papa said, patting my arm. "We know it's hard, but you have to give people a chance."

They didn't give *us* a chance, I protested to myself, and Mama, as if she'd heard me thinking, said, "Sometimes you have to give others what they won't give you. Sometimes they're just afraid."

I wanted to ask why they would be scared of us, when

Papa pulled Mama onto his knee and said, "These cookies are killers, woman."

"Sure enough," I agreed, hoping for more.

"We'll have to keep them a secret," Billie joined in, finally coming out of his dark mood. "The army might want to draft her as a secret weapon."

Mama laughed and said, "Thank you very much, but no more cookies until later." She slapped Papa's hand and took the plate away. Then she said, a little shy about complimenting herself, "The nuts made a difference, don't you think?"

We all nodded, our mouths full.

"It was lucky that Harry Slater came selling just as I was mixing the dough," she explained.

Billie and I stopped chewing and looked at each other, our eyes wide. Mama had bought the walnuts from Old Hairy! We managed to leave the kitchen fast and ran outside gagging and choking, certain we wouldn't live to see another day. We knew in our hearts that Mama would never want to feed us anything that might be poisoned, but Mama didn't seem to understand about Old Hairy, and we figured she never would.

Old Hairy had been around for as long as I could remember. And for as long as I could remember, seeing

him had made me think of nothing else but running, running for my life.

He was big, but he walked lightly, almost like he didn't weigh anything, almost like a ghost. He lived in a little cabin in the woods. That wasn't so unusual. Nobody in Mayfield Crossing had much. Mr. Wood's new Studebaker station wagon was the most exciting thing anybody'd brought home since Mr. Cleary won their color TV in a sweepstakes. Most of the fathers worked in the saw mill. But not Old Hairy. He sold things. Walnuts, berries, and things he made, like foot stools, picture frames, or Christmas wreaths.

"He makes an honest living," Mama would say.

But there was that hatchet. Dillon's brother Lucky, who left Mayfield to join the Navy, and Frank Sherman, who died the same year of pneumonia, told us about Old Hairy and his hatchet a long time ago. They said one day, when they knew Old Hairy was away picking berries, they went to his cabin and peeked in a window.

"There, lying on the table in plain sight, was the sharpest-looking hatchet you ever saw," Frank said.

"And there was hair and blood all over it," Lucky added in a deep whisper.

We were on Clearys' porch at the time and in the dark, shaking in our shoes just listening to them tell it. Nobody talked about what it might mean. We just looked at each other in the moonlight.

I believed every word. We all did. And we believed that if we weren't careful, *our* hair and *our* blood would end up on that hatchet.

I tried to tell Mama about the hatchet, but she only said, "I wish you kids would leave that man alone. You have no business snooping around his house."

I started to say, "I wasn't snooping," but she might have asked who was, so I dropped it.

Fitch and Owen think Old Hairy was the reason Frank died in the first place. They said one night during a storm, Old Hairy showed up at the Shermans' house carrying Frank, soaking wet and passed out from "the demon rum," as the preacher would say. After that, Frank came down with pneumonia and never got better. They think Old Hairy must've done something to make Frank so sick. I didn't want to think about what. I tried not to think about Old Hairy much at all.

But he wasn't easy to forget. The minute you got your mind on something else—say like a bunch of ants having a picnic on a cube of sugar—Hairy'd pop out of nowhere and scare you so your heart'd fly straight up into your throat.

One morning last spring after breakfast, I stepped out the front door and found him asleep on the porch glider. I jumped about a mile into the air and ran inside screaming, "Mama! Papa! Old Hairy. He's—"

"Calm down. He's no one to be afraid of," Mama said,

as I grabbed her tight around the waist. She brushed my bangs back with her hand. I could let her do that all day.

"Just let him be. He'll go home soon," Papa said, not even looking away from his newspaper.

I couldn't believe it. How could they be so calm about the Hatchet Man sleeping right on our porch?

I sat down with Mama, outraged. "What's wrong with him? Why isn't he home sleeping in his own bed?"

"There's nothing wrong with Harry. He's an original, that's all," she said, smiling.

"An original? Old Hairy?"

"First of all," Mama said, with a disapproving look, "Harry Slater isn't much older than I am. You don't call me 'Old Mama,' do you?" I shook my head, scared at just the thought of what would happen if I ever did.

"He just looks older because he has gray hair," Mama explained. "His hair was a nice auburn before he went into the Army. But, when he got back after the war, his hair had gone all gray."

"What made it change color?"

"Who knows?" Mama said. "Some terrible things happen in times of war."

"I still don't see why he's an original."

"Well," Mama paused, as if she wanted to make sure she was putting her words together right, then she said, "He has a special talent for making something useful out

of what seems to be nothing. Even as a boy he was never afraid to be different. Sometimes he drinks too much but, well, he's always had his own way of living."

I leaned my head on Mama's knee and tried to understand. But all I could do was tug my pigtail and wish Old Hairy's way of living didn't bring him to our front porch.

❧ Chapter Six

"You mean you actually *ate* walnuts that Old Hairy touched?" Fitch asked at lunch the next day. We were all squeezed together at one table, and Fitch was looking back and forth from Billie to me trying to decide which one of us looked likely to keel over first.

Billie confessed with a nod, but gave me a look that asked, *Why did you tell them? Nobody but us had to know.*

He was right. It just slipped out when I saw that Mama had put some of the cookies in our lunches.

"We didn't know until it was too late, and we spit them out," I explained, hoping to be redeemed.

"Your mom sure has a thing for Old Hairy," Owen teased.

"Mrs. Turner likes everybody," Mo said, leaning against me. I could always count on her.

"Yeah, and she makes really good cookies," Luke said.

We all looked longingly at the four huge chocolate-chip cookies.

"It's a shame," Alice sighed.

"It's a shame. It's a shame. But no one's to blame," Owen chanted.

"Hey, didn't you say you'd already swallowed some before you spit out the rest?" Luke asked. "And you guys are still alive. You didn't even get sick or anything, did you?"

Billie and I shook our heads.

"Well, maybe they're okay," Luke said, taking off his glasses, but keeping his eyes glued to the cookies. "Maybe Billie's mama is such a good person that the walnuts were purified the minute she touched 'em. Kinda like a small miracle."

We looked at each other. All wanting to believe, but still not sure if we should chance it. Luke had a way of talking you into things you could be sorry for later.

Then Alice said, "Your mama *is* the church-goin'est person I've ever seen."

Without another word we divided the cookies and ate them like there was no tomorrow. None of us had even eaten our sandwiches yet.

"I've been thinking," Billie started to say.

"Look out," Owen cut in, "Big Bill's thinkin'."

"Well, if we finish lunch early and get to the ball field

first, we can pick up a game ourselves and play. We don't need the Parkview kids."

"Yeah," said Luke, "we got along just fine without them before."

Nobody said anything more. Everybody was just rustling waxed paper, considering Billie's idea.

It was then that I heard someone behind me say, "I don't believe this. It's only the second day of school and I've lost my arithmetic book *and* forgotten my lunch."

I turned to see Ivy sitting at the next table where another girl was giving her half a cupcake. Ivy had gotten to the lunch room late, probably because of the book she'd lost, and it looked like everybody at the table had already eaten their sandwiches.

I elbowed Mo and said, "She needs more to eat than that."

"They're Parkview kids. What do we care?" Alice cut in. She was still mad about yesterday.

"Mama feeds hobos and she doesn't even know them," I said. "Besides, that Ivy girl sits right next to me in class, and she seems okay."

Mo shrugged. Alice ripped a bite out of her apple.

I looked at my sandwich. Peanut butter and jelly. I figured everybody liked peanut butter, so I went up to Ivy's table and said, "You can have half my sandwich."

Ivy looked surprised, then she opened her mouth to

say something, but another girl at her table blurted out, "You're crazy if you eat anything that trashy Mayfielder gives you. Who knows where it's been. It could even be rat meat or something."

"Is not," I said. "It's peanut butter and . . ."

"Yeah," said a boy beside Ivy. "You might not live to see the sun rise. Those coloreds are filthy."

Before I could read her face, Ivy turned away, saying, "No, thank you."

"I just thought . . ." I started to say, but I didn't finish. I knew if I said another word, the tears I was holding in would come right out.

As I was leaving, I heard the boy say, "What are you thanking her for, Ivy? She wasn't doing you a favor."

Then I heard commotion at our table and saw Luke, Fitch and Mo holding on to Billie. The look on my brother's face could have scared a dead man. It sure scared me.

I ran over and whispered, "Billie, remember what Papa said."

We got him to sit down, but he kept staring over at Ivy's table, beads of sweat popping out on his forehead.

"I'd like to go over there and show 'em they can't talk to us that way," Alice fumed.

"Me, too," Mo spat. She didn't sound like herself.

Finally, Billie relaxed. "You did right, Meg," he said. "They just don't have any manners."

"Yeah, they ain't worth it," Luke agreed.

"Forget it," I said, knowing I couldn't.

❧ *Chapter Seven*

"I'm the pitcher! Get off my mound!" Clayton Reed shouted to Billie.

We had started a pick-up game after lunch a couple of days later, just like we planned. We had been hanging around the swings, watching the Parkview kids play ball long enough. Today was our turn.

"You deaf or something, tar baby?" Clayton said as he marched across the field with about twenty kids following him.

Papa had warned us about fighting. But I felt sure something awful was about to happen. Billie looked ready to explode, but he didn't make a move. He might have been more afraid of our father than he was mad, but I think he just didn't want to let Papa down.

"I don't see your name on it," Alice announced. "This ball field is everybody's. And right now, we're using it."

"Yeah," Luke said, "First come, first served, so why don't you just get lost so we can finish our game."

"Make us," Clayton said. He hadn't pulled my hair since the first day, but I'd come to know that he had pulled it to be mean, not for fun. Now he was asking for a fight.

I glanced at Mo and could tell she was as scared as I was. We all stood around the pitcher's mound, eyeing each other—Mayfield kids and Parkview kids, waiting for someone to start something.

"Lordy," Dillon exclaimed, pointing toward home plate, "there's Old Hairy." Good ol' Dillon. We all owed him our lives. His eagle eye had saved us from Hairy a thousand times.

Everybody, even the Parkview kids, turned to look. There was Old Hairy, wearing those same faded overalls but a different shirt, watching us through the wire back-stop. He looked hot and sweaty, like he'd walked a long way, and he had his knapsack on his back.

"Shoot," Billie said, "how'd he get here?" My brother was right about most things, but he'd been dead wrong about Hairy not finding us at the new school.

"You know that guy?" Clayton asked, forgetting his challenge.

"No," Luke, Fitch, and Alice said all at once.

But it was too late to deny. Dillon had claimed Old Hairy as ours the minute he recognized him. And I could

see the sorry in Dillon's eyes. He must have felt as bad as I did telling about the cookies.

"You sure he's not your daddy?" Clayton said, laughing. He studied Hairy a moment, then frowned and said, "Hey, isn't he the Hatchet Man?"

Some other Parkview kids started saying things like, "the Hatchet Man," "He's supposed to be crazy," and "I heard he kills animals with a hatchet and eats them raw." I'd never heard anything like that. How did *they* know about Hairy?

"Figures he'd be from Mayfield." Clayton said. He tried to sound tough, but I could tell he was nervous. Billie picked up on it, too.

"Yeah, Old Hairy's from Mayfield," Billie said. "He keeps his bloody hatchet in that knapsack he's carryin' and he'll use it on more than animals if he has a mind to."

Clayton and the rest of the Parkview kids started to walk out across second base toward the school. "He's nothing but trash, like all you Mayfielders!" Clayton yelled.

"He isn't trash," I called, feeling braver as they hurried off the field. "Old Hairy's an original."

Billie looked at me, surprised, and laughed. "I wish Mama'd heard that."

Luke pulled my pigtail, teasing, and the rest of the Mayfield gang laughed.

They figured I'd said it just to get the last word, and

that was mostly true. But part of me was sticking up for Old Hairy because, whether he'd meant to or not, he'd done us a favor.

I looked back across home plate. Old Hairy was gone. I wasn't exactly sorry he'd left, but for the first time in my life I was glad he'd come. And for the first time since we'd come to Parkview, we played a little ball on the thick green grass of our new school field.

❧ *Chapter Eight*

I asked Billie not to tell Mama what I'd said about Old Hairy being an original. If I knew Mama, she might decide to invite him to supper or something. And I still didn't want to come within a mile of him.

That evening Fitch and Owen came to our bedroom window and were talking with Billie and me about school.

"Owen got a hundred percent on a spelling quiz we had today," Fitch told us, standing on tiptoes. Both he and Owen were short, but he was so proud he looked tall just then.

"Fitch only missed two." Owen propped his foot against the house. "It was only a practice test."

"So Miss Derry wrote Owen's name on the board with another kid who'd only missed one," Fitch went on. "A white kid. But the kid stood up and asked her to erase his name."

"Why?" I asked, pulling myself further onto the windowsill. Mrs. Sherman whistled for them to come home, but Fitch and Owen acted like they didn't even hear.

"He made Miss Derry think he was embarrassed to have his name up," Fitch explained. "But I heard him whisper to another white kid that he didn't want to be associated with us. With 'coloreds' is what he said." Fitch broke a stick in half.

It got quiet. There was something hanging in the air. Billie hadn't said a word. Owen had stopped talking, too, so I knew things weren't right. It was scary. We could always talk about things before. But we just stayed there—Billie and me leaning out the window, and Fitch and Owen against the house, watching the sun set. Finally, Mrs. Sherman whistled again, and Fitch and Owen ran home.

Later, in bed, I couldn't stop thinking about Owen. It was awful what had happened to him. But what really kept me awake were those two words—"white kid." I had never heard any of the Shermans talk that way before, or anybody in Mayfield. It gave me a pain in my chest I can't describe.

Next morning after Saturday chores, Billie and I went out to get some of the kids, but the Crossing was de-

serted. You'd have thought there'd been an air raid. The Clearys were visiting their grandma, Dillon was hunting with his dad, and the twins were grounded for staying out after their curfew the night before.

We wanted to explain to Mr. and Mrs. Sherman that it was partly our fault, that we were talking about something really important. But, on second thought, we knew Fitch and Owen wouldn't want us to. If things had been reversed, we wouldn't have wanted them to. So we went back home.

"Let's work on your village," Billie said.

"Sure enough?" I asked, uncertain that he meant it. Usually I had to beg him to do such things.

When I was little, we used to just make dirt roads for our miniature cars, but then we'd started setting up little houses from Billie's train set and adding some little farm animals I had. Sometimes we used rocks and sticks to stand for things, like corrals or benches. Once we even dug up johnny-jump-ups and buttercups and replanted them to make a park.

Mo and I had done some work the week before and it hadn't rained since then, so Billie and I didn't have to start from scratch. Billie took the toy beach shovel and started to scrape the roads to make them smooth again. I put three cars down on a section he had finished, then decided to make a pool for the park. I dug a hole

and fit a jar lid in so the top was even with the ground. I was cleaning up the area around the pool, planning to fill it with water, when a shadow blocked the sunlight.

I looked up. I stopped breathing. Old Hairy was standing right there watching me. He was so close I could have reached out and touched him. Worse than that, he could have touched me.

"Run, Meg!"

I was frozen in place looking straight at Old Hairy. The sun was behind him, so I couldn't see much. Only his big dark shape.

I thought I heard him start to say something just as Billie yanked my arm and we ran toward the house. I fell up the porch steps, climbing the last two on all fours with Billie pushing me from behind.

Then we charged inside, slamming the door behind us, and peeked out a window. Old Hairy just stood there looking at us, then he stooped down by our cars.

"What's he doin'?" I whispered, even though I didn't have to. Papa was at the store and Mama was in the cellar doing laundry.

We couldn't see what Hairy was up to but, at one point, he put his hand in his pocket. Finally, he stood up and looked at the house. Then he lifted his hand, like he did that day he broke up our last game of the summer. We

ducked behind the curtains. After a minute, Billie peeked out. "He's leaving. Come on."

"He took our cars!" I exclaimed, dashing with Billie to the scene of the crime.

But I was wrong. Our metal cars were right where we'd left them. On the dirt road behind them were two more cars made of walnut shells. Each had little pencil-eraser wheels with toothpicks for axles. I had never seen anything like them. There was a little red "B" painted on one and a blue "M" on the other.

"Glory," Billie said, scratching his head.

I couldn't help laughing. And I wondered what Old Hairy might have said if I'd stayed to hear.

❧ Chapter Nine

"You should have seen her," Dillon said Monday at the bus stop. "She had the biggest, prettiest eyes you ever saw."

"Did you shoot her?" Luke asked, winking at the rest of us. We all knew the answer.

"Naw, we were hunting ground hogs. It won't be doe season for a couple months."

We loved Dillon's hunting stories. As usual, he didn't kill anything. We used to think Dillon just couldn't shoot straight. But we had all come to realize that he would never kill anything on purpose. He just liked going camping with his dad and seeing the animals. The only real shooting he did was with a Brownie camera.

"Oh, no," Mo suddenly moaned, looking at her arms. They were red and splotchy. "I must have gotten poison ivy picking berries at Gram's." She started to twitch. We

all knew how it was. Once you know you have it, you feel itchy all over.

When we got to school, Mr. Stanley sent Mo to the nurse. I missed her the minute she left the room.

I caught Ivy's eye. She looked back at Clayton, then faced straight ahead. I wished I knew what she was thinking.

Last Friday, Mr. Stanley had mentioned that we were going to be studying the fifty states. He said we might want to test ourselves over the weekend, just for fun, to see how many state names we could remember.

"I told you Friday that I wasn't going to test you today on the states, and I'm not," he said. "But I thought we'd have a little contest. Don't worry. No grades."

This was my lucky day. The year before, at Mayfield School, our third-grade class learned a song about the states for our spring concert. We practiced that song so many times I was singing it in my sleep.

Even though I knew I could never forget it, I sang it to Mama on Saturday just in case, and I still knew every state in alphabetical order. Then Mo and I sang it again together on Sunday. I felt bad that she wasn't going to be in on the contest.

After we had gotten paper and put our names on it, Mr. Stanley said, "Ready? Begin."

I started with "Alabama" and sang it all the way through in my head, writing as fast as I could.

"Pencils down," Mr. Stanley said just as I was finishing the "g" in Wyoming. "Now," he continued, "the last person in each row, bring your paper to the first person in the row, and everyone else pass your paper to the person behind you."

I tugged my pigtail. Clayton would be checking my paper. Then I relaxed and felt kind of good. It would kill him that I had a perfect paper.

Mr. Stanley started calling off state names in alphabetical order, giving everyone enough time to check through their lists.

The curly-haired girl in front of me, whose name was Jane, had thirty-three states. I thought that was pretty good considering that nobody had really studied. Then I felt a little guilty. Maybe it wasn't fair that I knew that song.

"Mr. Stanley," Clayton suddenly called out. "I think I caught myself a cheater."

Everybody looked at me. I turned toward Clayton. He was grinning like he'd just answered the $64,000 Question.

Mr. Stanley frowned. "Now, wait a minute, Clayton. That's a very serious accusation."

"I know, sir," Clayton replied. "But she must have a cheat sheet because they're all in alphabetical order. She wasn't even smart enough to mix them up." Mr. Stanley was standing right beside us by then and Clayton handed him my paper.

He looked at the paper and asked, not like he was accusing me or anything, "Margaret, would you like to tell us your side of this?"

I wanted to, but I was so mad, I knew I'd cry if I opened my mouth. My eyes were already filling up. Mr. Stanley must have seen because he touched my shoulder and led me out of the classroom. Before the door closed, some kids were talking and I heard someone say, "That dumb Mayfielder's in for it now."

Mr. Stanley stuck his head back in the door and shushed the class. Then he gave me his handkerchief. It was so clean and fancy with a blue "S" sewn on it, I felt funny about using it. "Don't worry," he said, "I have eleven more just like it."

I smiled a little and blew my nose.

"Now," he said, "tell me."

"I don't know. Maybe it *was* cheating," I said. Then I told him about the song.

Mr. Stanley chuckled, put his hands on my shoulders, and said firmly, "You did *not* cheat, Meg. Cheating involves dishonesty. Something you learned in the past paid off today, that's all. And you can feel good about that."

"Mo Cleary knows the song, too," I said, not wanting to take all the credit.

"Well, then, you both should feel proud," Mr. Stanley

said. "And your teacher would be proud that you remembered something good from last year. Every teacher wants that."

I handed him his handkerchief, and he stuck it right back in his pocket, even though I'd blown my nose on it.

I went back to my seat and Mr. Stanley explained the whole thing to the class.

Clayton whispered, "You dirty liar." Then he raised his hand and said, "Mr. Stanley, do you think she could sing this song for the whole class? Maybe we'd *all* like to learn it."

My face got hot. It was a challenge, I knew. Mr. Stanley knew it, too.

"If you're asking Margaret to prove herself, I don't think that's necessary."

I was glad that Mr. Stanley believed me, but I wanted to show that Clayton Reed. "I don't mind singing it," I said.

Mr. Stanley nodded.

I marched to the front of the classroom and sang the whole song. Not just the states part, but all the rest about the fifty states being from thirteen original colonies, about the fifty stars in the flag and everything. I sang the best I could, with feeling, like my music teacher always told us to. And when I finished, everybody clapped.

It was clear that I had won the contest. Mr. Stanley gave me a jigsaw puzzle of the fifty states.

"I wish I had one for Mo. I must say, I wasn't prepared for you two," he said, laughing.

As I walked back to my desk, I looked right at Clayton and kept staring at him. His face was redder than I thought a person's could get. I flashed him a fake smile before sitting down.

"Clayton, I believe you owe Margaret an apology," Mr. Stanley said. "Normally I would ask that you do it privately, but your accusation was a public one; therefore, your apology should be also."

There was a long silence. Then Clayton, looking at his desk top the whole time, mumbled, "Sorry I said she was cheating."

"Don't tell *me*. Tell *her*," Mr. Stanley insisted.

Clayton sighed. I almost felt sorry for him. It was like it was the hardest thing he ever had to do.

"Sorry I said you were cheating," he finally said.

He never looked at me or said my name, but I knew it was the best I'd get, so I said, "Okay."

Mr. Stanley started pointing out states on a huge map on the wall. I was glad we were getting back to normal.

I was putting my puzzle away when I saw Ivy looking at me, and this time she didn't turn away. She smiled. It

was a shy smile, like she wasn't sure how I felt. I smiled back, and hoped she'd know.

But the good feeling was ruined by Clayton, who leaned forward, pulled my pigtail hard, and said, "Just wait until recess."

❧ *Chapter Ten*

"He apologized in front of the whole class?" Mo asked with a grin, as we hurried out for recess. Her arms were pink with calamine lotion.

I was telling her all about the contest, and keeping a lookout for Clayton. I didn't know what he'd do, but whatever it was, I didn't want it to come by surprise.

It did anyway. I turned my head to check behind me and the next thing I knew Mo was shouting, "Meg! Look out!" and I hit the ground. Clayton had rammed right into me. He moved like he was going to jump on me, but I got to my feet and ran. I was a pretty fast runner and it helped that I was scared. But Clayton's legs were longer and he was as mad as I was scared. I could hear his shoes pounding the ground behind me, and gaining. Finally, he got close enough to grab one of my pigtails and put me on the ground again. It hurt so bad I forgot everything Papa had said and was ready to fight back.

Clayton started to come at me and I was putting my feet up to kick him off, when somebody jumped on him from behind. It was Billie. They both fell over, then they got to their feet and stood, fists up, yelling at each other.

"Wanna fight somebody?" Billie shouted, "I'll fight you. But lay another hand on my sister and I'll kill you."

"I'll do what I want to your pickaninny sister, and I'll beat the black offa you, too!" Clayton hollered.

Billie went in swinging and Clayton started punching back.

By now, kids had gathered and were screaming. And I was feeling scared for Billie. Not that he'd get hurt bad, but that if somebody didn't stop him, maybe he *would* kill Clayton. He was madder than I'd ever seen him.

"Billie!" I cried, trying to get up, hurting all over.

"Here comes Mr. Perkins!" someone called. "Mrs. Carmichael, too!"

Clayton stopped throwing punches the second he heard that teachers were coming, but Billie either hadn't heard or didn't care. He belted Clayton in the stomach and started to hit him again, but I ran to Billie, threw my arms around him from behind, and held on.

He was trembling, then in an instant I felt him relax and he turned around and hugged me tight. My back hurt from the fall, but I didn't care. I could have stood there being held forever if Mr. Perkins hadn't grabbed Billie's

shirt collar and shouted, "Hey, boy! Just what do you think you're doing?"

One of Billie's buttons popped off.

"Hey!" I couldn't help saying and stooped down to pick it up from the ground. I wanted to say more, but I stopped myself. I knew Mama and Papa would skin me alive for being disrespectful. Still, it didn't seem right that Mr. Perkins should be so rough with Billie. Like he was some kind of criminal.

Clayton was bent over holding his stomach, and talking to Mrs. Carmichael.

Mr. Perkins yanked Billie's shirt again, then grabbed my arm with his other hand and said, "You two need to have a talk with the principal."

"You had better come too, Clayton," Mrs. Carmichael said, patting his shoulder.

"Yes, ma'am," Clayton said, acting as innocent as a preacher's son.

As they took us into the school building, Mr. Perkins said to Mrs. Carmichael, "Do you want to bet this won't be the first time something like this happens?"

She nodded and said, "I knew these Mayfield kids would be nothing but trouble."

They expected us to be bad, just like Mrs. Sherman had said. It wasn't right. I held back a sob, but couldn't stop the tears.

* * *

"This is a school, *not* a war zone," Mr. Callahan, the principal, told us from behind his huge desk. "Now, what started this?"

"He threatened to kill me," Clayton blurted out, which wasn't exactly true. Then he *really* lied and made it sound like we ganged up on him.

"I was just walking, minding my own business, when that . . . that boy," he said, pointing to Billie, "jumped on my back. Then after I was down, his sister kicked me in the stomach, so I fought back. It was self-defense."

"Why would they attack you?" Mr. Callahan asked.

"Don't ask *me*," Clayton said, throwing his hands in the air. "We never had trouble before those Mayfielders came."

The principal was quiet a minute, then he turned to Billie and me. "Is that the way it happened?"

The two of us just sat there. Telling—even on someone like Clayton—wasn't our way. Mr. Callahan looked at us hard. I could see a big paddle in the corner behind his desk. It looked old and worn like it had swatted a zillion kids. If Parkview was anything like Mayfield, fighting was serious enough for getting the wood.

Finally Billie said, "It won't happen again, Mr. Callahan, sir."

"You are very right about that," he said. "And what about you, Miss Turner? It's bad enough that these boys were fighting, but you're a young lady." When Mr. Callahan frowned, it looked like he had one big eyebrow drawn over his eyes with no space in between.

I tried not to say anything, but I couldn't help it. "Billie was just protecting me," I said.

"Meg," Billie said.

Mr. Callahan shook his head at Billie and said to me, "Go on."

I tugged my pigtail and I looked down at my lap. "In Mayfield . . . we don't tell on each other," I said quietly. "That's why Billie isn't talking."

"I see."

"But it isn't right for Clayton to say what he did either."

Clayton stood up like he was going to argue, but Mr. Callahan put his hand up like a traffic cop and he sat back down.

"I understand how you feel. But it would help if I had all the facts," Mr. Callahan said.

I almost looked at Billie to see if his eyes approved, then I changed my mind. I didn't want to know because I knew I had to tell it anyway.

I took a deep, shaky breath. Then I started with the fifty states and had just gotten to the part where Clayton

pulled my hair and knocked me down on the playground, when Clayton blurted out, "She's a filthy liar."

"You're the liar," Billie yelled back.

"Who are you going to believe?" Clayton asked Mr. Callahan. "Me, or them coloreds from Mayfield? Even my father says they're all liars." His voice got quieter at the end, like he might be saying something he shouldn't to the principal.

Mr. Callahan was standing now, his thick eyebrows lower on his forehead. He looked dead at Clayton and said, "Who these children are or where they come from is not a matter of concern to me. What I'm interested in here is the truth."

He sat back down and nodded for me to finish telling what happened. When I got to the end I said, "So Billie wouldn't have been fighting, but well, he's my brother."

Mr. Callahan didn't answer. I figured he didn't want to say it was okay to fight. He couldn't. He was the principal. But I got the feeling that Mr. Callahan understood. He straightened some papers on his desk, thinking. I eyed the wood. He was going to use it. I knew it. We had broken the rules. He didn't have a choice. He picked up the paddle and went into the assistant principal's office. I heard them talking, then Mr. Callahan called us in one by one.

Clayton went first. He got three swats, hard ones, I

could tell. He was bawling when he left. Billie was next. I could hear them talking for a while, then three swats again, but quieter. Billie didn't cry. I knew he wouldn't.

"Miss Turner?" Mr. Callahan said. I was scared, but I wanted to be brave like Billie. I walked in. The assistant principal was leaning back in his desk chair like this was something that happened every day, like the morning announcements or the lunch-time bell.

"How many swats do you think you'll need so that this won't happen again?" Mr. Callahan asked.

I didn't know what to say. At first I thought I didn't need *any* swats. But then I confessed, "Well, I guess I didn't have to sing the fifty states song. I guess I just wanted to make Clayton mad."

"One swat?" Mr. Callahan asked.

I nodded, leaned over with my hands on my knees, and closed my eyes tight while he swung the big paddle. I never thought I'd smile getting the wood, but it felt as light as Mama's hand sending me off to bed.

When I turned around, Mr. Callahan's face was serious, but his eyes were smiling.

"Let *that* be a lesson to you," he said firmly.

I started to say, *That didn't hurt at all!* But he put his finger to his lips like it was a secret.

We walked back through his office to the door. "One more thing," he said.

"Yes, sir?"

He stooped down so I could look straight at him. "Come back and talk to me sometime. I'd like to hear more about Mayfield Crossing."

On the way home from the bus stop, Billie told me Mr. Callahan had asked him the same question about the swats. "I told him I'd take what Clayton got, but I think he went easy on me."

"He sure went easy on *me*," I said, "but I got the feeling that Mr. Callahan wouldn't want us to tell anybody."

"Yeah," Billie agreed. "We shouldn't tell Mama and Papa about the fight, either. It would only get us into more trouble, and they would worry about something they can't do anything about anyway."

He wanted me to swear with a spit handshake not to tell. He said we had to work things out ourselves. I didn't see how we could, but I swore anyway.

It turned out to be a wasted promise because the minute we walked into the house Mama said, "The principal called."

❧ *Chapter Eleven*

"Mr. Callahan explained what happened today," Mama said, stirring a pot of navy beans.

Billie and I looked at each other. We hadn't thought he would, but I guessed it was another one of those things a principal doesn't have a choice about.

"Now," Mama said. She put the lid on the pot and turned to face us. "I want to hear it from you."

I knew what that meant. We'd talk about it, and then we'd get a spanking. It was a standing rule. If we did something bad enough to get paddled at school, then we got it at home, too.

"Just lick us now and get it over with," I said.

Mama brushed my bangs back with her hand and said softly, "I'm not going to spank you. Not after what Mr. Callahan said."

I couldn't believe it. It was a first.

"I just want you to talk to me about this whole situation at Parkview. I know there are things going on that you haven't told me or your father."

"It's okay, Mama," Billie insisted.

Mama looked me right in the eyes. I looked at my shoelaces.

"Please, Mama," Billie begged, "let it be for now."

Mama studied us both for a minute, then she did what Billie asked. She let it be. "For now," she added. I knew that meant we'd have to talk about it when Papa came home.

Billie and I went out and sat on the back porch swing. The Clearys came over to see if we wanted to play ball. Billie just shook his head as Dillon and the twins walked up the porch steps.

"Did you get it again because of the fight today?" Alice was asking. Luke shushed her.

"No," I answered. "Mama said we'll talk about it later."

Everybody had seen most of the fight, but I told them about everything else, except the swats and our secret with Mr. Callahan.

"Wow," Luke said. "I wish our teacher was as nice as yours, Meg. Don't you, Billie?"

"Yeah."

Billie hadn't told me much about Mrs. Carmichael at all, only that she was hard.

"Is she mean?" Mo asked.

"She pretends to be nice," Luke explained. "But you can tell that she doesn't like us Mayfield kids. She said we'll all have to get used to—" he pushed his glasses down and wrinkled his nose to give us a picture of how she looked— *"higher standards.* And it's worse for Billie," he went on, and told all about how their teacher said it wouldn't be so easy for Billie to make A's at Parkview. Luke mocked her using a high, scratchy voice. "But your people have come a long way. I'm sure you'll do fine."

Billie rolled his eyes.

"I get the same feeling from Miss Derry," Alice said, looking at Owen. "When you got the best spelling grade, remember how she checked your paper about three times, like she couldn't believe it?"

"Didn't you tell us she put your name on the board?" I asked.

"Yeah," Fitch said, "but not until after she was sure his mark was for real. She even asked him to spell two of the hardest words out loud."

"I knew she was checking to see if I'd cheated somehow, but she tried not to make it seem that way," Owen said. "She just said a lot of people had missed those words and that I should remind the class how to spell them, even though all anybody had to do was check the darn book."

Alice sighed. "Nobody wants us there." She slid her back down the side of the house and sat on the porch floor.

Luke plopped into a lawn chair and stared at the ceiling. Fitch and Owen sat on the top porch step, looking away from the house. Dillon stood behind them, leaning against the side of the house. I was on the porch swing between Billie and Mo. It was dead quiet. Mo put her head on my shoulder.

In a little while she said, "Mr. Stanley's nice."

"And Mr. Callahan," I added.

"And we did get to play on the field the other day," Luke said.

We were all looking for the silver lining in the dark cloud over Parkview School.

After Papa came home, we had our talk. He smiled a little when I told him about what happened with the fifty states, but he said, "It *was* wrong of you to be so smug. It only made matters worse."

"I know, Papa," I said, unable to look at his eyes.

He patted my leg. "Yes, I know you know. Just try not to forget what you've learned."

Then he turned to Billie. "Was there any time during the fight that you could have walked away?"

"He was beating up on Meg, Papa," Billie said.

"Yes, I know. And you were right to defend her. But think about it. Could you have ended it sooner?"

Billie was quiet, then he said, "Yes, sir."

I didn't know what he was talking about. "When?" I asked.

"After I jumped on Clayton and we were yelling at each other. I could have quit, but he said that stuff that made me mad."

I remembered what Clayton had said. People always say words can't hurt you, but that isn't true. They can hurt worse than a punch in the eye.

But Papa understood. He didn't punish us. He said, "You've never had hatred in your hearts. Don't let them put it there now. If you do, then *they* win."

Mama squeezed us both. "You just do what you've always done. Be your best."

Long after bedtime, I still couldn't sleep. I could hear something on television about the election for president. I knew Mama and Papa were hoping a man named Kennedy would win. "He would be good for this country," Mama had said.

If this Kennedy did become president, I wondered if he could come to Parkview and straighten things out.

Maybe. He must be a good man or Mama and Papa wouldn't vote for him.

Even though Billie was across the room and facing the wall, I was sure he was awake, too.

"Billie?"

He didn't answer for a while and I thought maybe I was wrong, maybe he *was* asleep. Then he said, "Papa always told us it was wrong to fight, but he never said how right it'd feel to hit somebody like Clayton."

"Did it really feel good?"

"Yeah."

"What are we gonna do, Billie?"

"We'll work it out."

"But how? How can we work it out with kids who think we're trash?"

"I'm not sure," he whispered, turning over to face me in the dark. "But Papa's right. It's not right for us to be hatin' them and them to be hatin' us."

We were quiet for a bit. I got this picture in my head of what it could be like if we all got along.

"Wouldn't it be great if we could play a real game of baseball with the kids from Parkview?"

"Yeah." It was quiet again, then suddenly Billie sat up and said, "Maybe we can, Meg."

"Are you kids still awake in there?" Mama called.

I waited until I knew Mama wasn't listening anymore

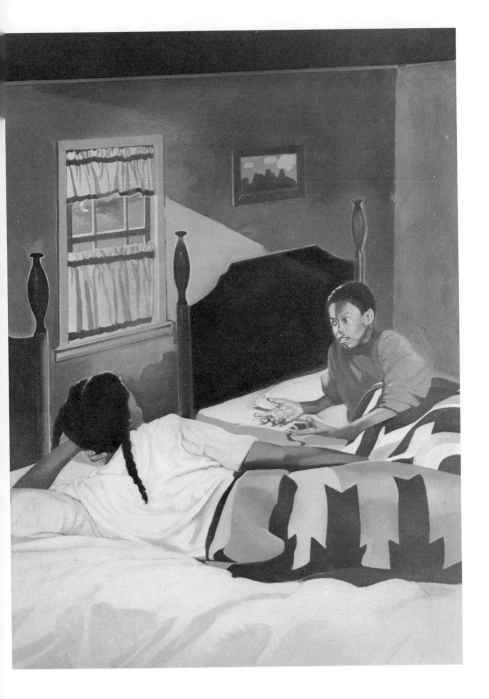

and whispered, "What are you talking about? How're we gonna get them to play *us?*"

"Let me think," Billie said with hope in his voice. "We'll talk about it tomorrow."

I heard Owen's voice echo in my head. *Look out. Big Bill's thinkin'.*

I pulled the covers up and closed my eyes tight. Mama always said just wishing a thing wouldn't make it happen, but I figured with me wishing and Billie thinking, anything might.

❧ *Chapter Twelve*

When I woke up, Billie's bed was made and he was gone. Mama said he'd gotten ready for school early and gone over to Clearys'.

Shoot, I thought. I hadn't heard a thing. When he wanted to, Billie could be quieter than a cat. I was dying to know what he was planning. I got dressed as fast as I could and started to rush out, but Mama called me back for breakfast.

"Aw, Mama, just this once." I stood at the table and gulped down my juice, ready to make my escape.

Papa folded down his newspaper and gave me *the look.* It was a warning.

I sat down and ate my cereal. Papa nodded and went back to his paper. When I'd finished, Mama kissed my forehead and hugged me.

"You take care today, you hear?"

"Yes, ma'am," I answered, as she handed me my lunch and shooed me out the front door.

One step later I caught my breath and jumped back inside. Old Hairy was asleep on the porch again. What did he think this was, a hotel?

Mama had already gone back into the kitchen, and I started to run after her. But something made me go back and peek at Hairy through the screen door. He looked funny, sort of smiling in his sleep, but snoring like a freight train. At the same time he seemed peaceful, lying in the shade of Mama's pretty purple morning glories strung from the porch rail, with his hands folded together on his belly.

I opened the door quietly and tiptoed right up next to him. There were some reddish-brown stains on his hands, and for a second I thought it might be blood. But he smelled a little like turpentine, so I figured it was the varnish he used for his wood crafts. He smelled like sweat and whiskey, too, and he *was* hairy, but he didn't really look like a werewolf. His whiskers looked soft and shiny, like if I touched them they'd feel like silk. Still, if he had opened his eyes, I might've died of fright.

I squeezed my own eyes shut and slowly opened my lunch bag. I reached inside, wishing that paper bags didn't make so much noise, that I could be as quiet as Billie. After what seemed like a hundred minutes, I finally pulled out

my peanut butter sandwich. I put it right beside Hairy, near his face so he'd see it when he woke up. Then I ran to the bus stop.

"Meg really gave me the idea," Billie was saying when I arrived.

"What idea?" I wanted to know.

"We're going to challenge Clayton and the Parkview kids to a baseball game," Luke said.

"They'll never play us," Alice grumbled, shaking her head. I was thinking the same thing. They didn't want to play ball with us before, why would they now?

"Yes, they will," Billie insisted. "Because we won't be asking to play *with* them. We're gonna tell them we want to play *against* them for the school championship."

"Yeah," Dillon said, smiling. "They'll have to agree or it will look like they're scared we might beat 'em, which we will."

"Even if they *do* play us, how's that gonna change anything?" I asked. "If we win, they'll hate us more, and if we lose they'll make fun of us worse than ever."

"I don't think so, Meg," Billie said. "If we win, maybe they won't like us, but they'll have to respect us, and that's somethin'."

"What if we lose?" Owen asked.

"Don't know. It's a risk, I guess. And maybe everybody doesn't wanna take it."

"We should vote," Mo said.

"Okay," Luke asked with his hand already in the air. "How many want to challenge the Parkview kids to a championship game, win or lose?"

Billie's hand was up right away, along with Dillon's. I looked at Mo and we raised ours together. Alice's was up and waving. We all faced the twins.

Fitch looked like he wanted to go along, but he held back, studying Owen. I knew what was happening. Fitch knew that Owen would do what he did, but he also figured that Owen was scared to play. He didn't want to hurt our chances of winning.

I could tell Owen wanted to play, and I wanted him to. It wouldn't seem right without us all together.

"Come on, Owen," I said. "Remember what you said— 'We're gonna hang 'em on the line, press 'em, and stack 'em up high'?"

Owen laughed. "No," he said, "it's—'hang 'em out to dry, iron 'em, and stack 'em in neat little piles.' "

Fitch slapped Owen's back, grabbed his hand and raised it high in the air.

It looked like we were gonna play some ball.

❧ Chapter Thirteen

"So what do you say?" Billie asked Clayton at recess. "Do you want to play us for the school championship or not?"

As usual, we were divided, with Mayfield kids standing behind Billie on one side of the pitcher's mound and Parkview kids behind Clayton on the other.

Clayton stood glaring. I could tell he didn't trust us.

"Forget it," Luke said, signaling us to walk away. "He's scared of losin'."

We played along and started to leave, knowing Clayton would have to agree now. It was like one of those duels in the Three Musketeers' time. If someone slapped you in the face with a glove, you had to fight, even if you knew you'd get killed or you didn't feel like killing anybody. In those days, it was better to die because you were brave than to live because you were chicken.

"Okay," Clayton finally said. "We'll play. But this is

going to be a real championship game, so everything has to be by the rules."

"That's the way we want it," Billie said. "Fair."

We decided to play the game on Saturday afternoon on the school ball field, figuring we could get somebody's mom or dad to drive us over from the Crossing. I was hoping to get another ride in Mr. Wood's new Studebaker.

That afternoon we met at the old Mayfield School field to practice. First we had to decide what positions people would play.

"We only have eight players," Dillon reminded everyone.

"It doesn't matter," Alice declared. "We could beat them with seven."

We all cheered in agreement.

I'd play my usual position as catcher and Billie would pitch. Luke would play first base, with Dillon on second, and Owen on third, right beside Fitch who would be shortstop. Alice was to cover right field and Mo, left. The center field position was left open. Billie figured Dillon could help cover center, since he could run and could handle grounders. But Dillon wasn't sure. Fly balls were his weakness.

"I don't know, Billie," he said. "Maybe we should put Mo here. She's good with flies."

"Mo can play a little toward center, but you'll be okay,

Dillon," Billie said without a bit of question in his voice. "Don't worry."

We practiced every day that week after school. On Friday, Papa and Mr. Cleary came and hit some balls for us to field, and they substituted for players who were practicing their batting. Papa was slamming balls all over the place, giving everybody a chance to make a play.

When we went home that night, Papa helped us oil our gloves. Then after supper, Mama poured grape juice into four fancy glasses.

"To a good game tomorrow," Papa toasted.

We clinked our glasses together. "A good game," we all said, and drank. We were as ready as we were going to be.

On Saturday morning, Dillon's dad drove us to Parkview in his Studebaker, and I even got to ride up front next to the window. My pigtails were flying in the wind, and by the time we reached Parkview, I was ready to win that game.

"Are you sure you don't want me to stay to cheer you on?" Mr. Wood asked.

"No thanks, Dad," Dillon said.

We had all asked our parents not to come to watch. They would just make us nervous.

We piled out of that shiny new car and walked across

the field to the pitcher's mound to meet with Clayton and his team and decide who'd be batting first.

It looked like the whole school had turned out. There were kids all over the bleachers and standing around the edge of the field.

Clayton tossed the bat and Billie caught it to start the hand-over-hand. Whoever was left holding the end could bat first.

"Hey, wait a minute. Wait just one *cotton pickin' minute*," Clayton said loudly, smiling in a mean sort of way. Some kids on his team snickered.

"Didn't we say this game was going to be by the rules?" he said. "Don't you know anything at all about baseball?"

"What in blazes are you talking about?" Billie asked.

Clayton looked at some of the Parkview kids and smiled. "You can't play an official baseball game with only eight players."

Billie wiped the sweat from his forehead. "We're willing to play with a handicap and call it even."

"Doesn't matter what you're willing to do, Billie Boy. The rules say nine players. If you can't come up with nine in"—he looked at his watch—"ten minutes, then you forfeit, and *we* win."

"Yeah!" some Parkview kids yelled, but only some. Most were quiet, waiting to see what would happen next.

Someone on the bleachers yelled, "Aw, man! What *is* this?"

Another kid hollered, "On with the game!"

Clayton turned around and shouted, "Rules are rules!"

Billie motioned us to walk over toward third base with him. We huddled together.

"Anybody got any ideas?" he asked.

"We shoulda figured he'd pull somethin' like this," Alice said.

"Yeah, but right now we have to think what to do about it," Billie said.

I figured it was all over until my eye caught motion behind the backstop. It was Old Hairy. Before I even thought about it I said, "What if we ask Hairy?"

Everybody looked at me like I'd invited Frankenstein to dinner.

"Are you crazy, Meg?" Luke said, half laughing. "What's the matter with you?"

"Remember how fast he took the bases that time? He *is* from Mayfield, and I don't mind askin' him."

Everybody was protesting until Billie said, "Anybody got a better idea?"

Nobody said anything. I tugged my pigtail and started to walk toward the backstop. Suddenly I was feeling scared. It was like the Three Musketeers thing again. I didn't really know what Old Hairy would do, but I would

rather face a bloody hatchet than forfeit the game to Clayton Reed.

Just then Clayton stepped in front of me. "Where do you think you're going?" He looked over his shoulder at Hairy. "No way!" he said. "No grown-ups."

"That's not an official baseball rule," Fitch said, as the gang gathered around again. The Parkview players came close enough to hear, but they kept watching Hairy.

"You said a fair game," Clayton insisted. "What if I knew Mickey Mantle and brought him along? Would that be fair?"

We hated to admit it, but Clayton was right. It wouldn't be fair for a grown-up to play. Even Hairy.

Billie looked at his watch, then at us. His eyes said he was sorry, as if all this was his fault.

I looked across the field toward the bleachers. There were kids everywhere. Parkview kids.

I caught myself wishing again, even though I knew just wishing a thing wouldn't make it happen. *You have to make things happen*, Mama'd say. *Sometimes you have to take chances.*

Billie sighed and turned to Clayton, who hadn't stopped smiling since he walked onto the field, held out his hand, and said, "Well, it looks like we'll have to . . ."

"Wait!" I yelled. And I ran toward the bleachers, toward that head of short blond hair that reminded me so much of Dillon.

"Ivy?" I said. I didn't have to shout. I could tell she'd seen me coming and was looking right at me from the second row of the bleachers. Billie and Clayton and the whole gang had run over behind me.

"Ivy?" I said again.

Ivy glanced at a girl sitting next to her. The girl frowned and mouthed the words, "No way."

Ivy looked down at the ball glove in her hand.

It was so quiet I could hear my heart beating.

"She's not going to play for *you*," Clayton said, laughing.

Ivy punched the pocket of her glove, looked up at Clayton, and said, "Wanna bet?" She jumped down from her seat in the bleachers, ran over to Billie, and said, "I can play the outfield."

"You can't!" Clayton yelled, pushing some kids aside to stand in front of her. "You said you didn't want to play ball today."

"I changed my mind," Ivy said calmly.

Clayton kept hollering. "This is supposed to be Parkview kids against Mayfield kids. The championship. You *can't* play for them."

"Clayton," Ivy said, turning toward us, "Mayfield kids *are* Parkview kids."

"Yeah!" Mo and I cried together. Mo took her ball cap off and plunked it down on Ivy's head. Ivy flashed her that shy smile, same as she did me that day in class, then

she reached up, grabbed the brim of the hat and pulled it down over one eye.

Billie smiled at Ivy and punched her lightly on the shoulder. Then he looked at his watch and said to Clayton, "Time to play ball."

A couple of kids on the bleachers yelled, "Traitor," as Ivy ran onto the field, but some were clapping and cheering. They had come out today for the same thing we had, a ball game.

Clayton asked for five minutes to talk to his team and looked grateful when Billie agreed. It sounded like he was deciding who would play what position. I realized then that Clayton had known all along that we only had eight players. He hadn't planned on playing the game from the beginning.

While we waited, Billie dusted my catcher's mitt with a couple of fast balls, then Luke hit a hot line drive straight to center field.

"I got it," Ivy called, and she did.

"Good catch," Alice yelled.

"She's Ivy, but she sure ain't poison," Owen chattered.

"You got that right," a boy from Parkview joined in.

The Untouchable Turner had Fitch swinging at air, but finally he hit a grounder that took him to second base. Dillon warmed up on deck.

"They're pretty good," I heard a girl on the bleachers say, as Billie pitched another Turner.

I felt like jumping clean to the sky. I hardly even cared who won anymore because I knew there'd be other games—lots of them.

I was scooping up a ball that had gotten away from me when I got a glimpse of Hairy standing behind the backstop.

I pushed back my catcher's mask and looked him right in the eyes. The sunlight was shining just right, and I could see they were a pretty green color. "Hey, Mr. Slater," I said, putting my hand up. Harry smiled and raised his.

I pulled my mask back down and threw the ball to Billie. He was shaking his head and laughing, saying, "Wait 'til I tell Mama."

"No, Billie," I said. "Wait 'til *I* tell her."